To my friends Annie + George—

I AM TONY:
Homeless at the Jersey Shore

Thanks for helping the homeless!!.

DAVE TRANSUE

All the best - Dave

Also by Dave Transue: *Bounding up the Steps*

All characters and organizations appearing in this work are fictitious.
Any resemblance to real persons, living or dead, or organizations,
is purely coincidental. Characters, dialogue, incidents, and
organizations are entirely of the imagination of the author.

To the Lord God, my Savior…who came to this world poor and who had no home of His own as he ministered to the needy and infirmed, telling them, "Blessed are you who are poor, for yours is the Kingdom of God." Jesus also tells us in Matthew, "Foxes have holes, and birds of the air have nests, but the Son of Man has nowhere to lay his head."

To the homeless of our society…who live in the shadows, suffering daily challenges as they battle addiction, untreated mental illness, joblessness, weather, hunger, thirst, unaffordable rents, lack of healthcare, lack of clothing, lack of dignity and self-esteem, and all the things those of us who have food, clothing, shelter, and our physical needs addressed in great abundance will never understand. But for the grace of God, I would be in these same circumstances. Mother Teresa said it better than I ever could, "Each one of them is Jesus in disguise." How we treat the poor is how we would treat Jesus.

To our parents, Ed, June, Jack, Virgie…for your love and for instilling in us those values in life that matter most: faith, country, family, hard work, decency, Christian charity towards the less fortunate.

To my Harrisburg pal of over thirty years, Bob Keaton… you left us far too early. I will remember you the rest of my days. Thanks for all the laughs and a friendship I will always cherish.

To my fraternity brother and forever friend, Greg Gorddard, and my college friend, Valerie Lewandowski Geller, who cares so deeply about the poor...thank you from the bottom of my heart for reading my draft and providing constructive criticism.

And always to my wonderful wife...without whom I cannot imagine life.

All profits from book sales of *I am Tony: Homeless at the Jersey Shore* will go to Just B.E., a ministry—led by its founder and my friend, Rosemary MacMaster—which does a wonderful job at the Jersey Shore in providing the "basic essentials" to the homeless. For those readers who wish to donate directly to this terrific organization, Just B.E. can be found on Facebook at: https://www.facebook.com/justbasicessentials.
Your support will make a difference in the lives of the homeless of our communities.

About the Author

Dave published his first fictional novel, *Bounding up the Steps,* in 2018. Inspired to write while vacationing in Florida, the author woke up in the middle of the night. On hotel stationary, he scratched out the title, main characters, and an outline containing the basic plot. Over two years later, after intense writing and editing, he launched *Bounding up the Steps.*

After careers in real estate, the antiques business, and service in various legislative staff positions with the Pennsylvania General Assembly and serving in leadership positions with various charitable and nonprofit endeavors in the Harrisburg region, he and his wife, Christine, retired to live on the Jersey Shore in the magical little town of Ocean Gate. As a couple, they volunteer with local programs that serve the homeless and spoil their pit bull, Brownie, who they rescued from the streets.

CHAPTER ONE

From Tony's Journal
June 14, 2015
Day 32 of Homelessness

My name is Tony. Or more formally, Anthony Bennett Jankowski. My mother Maria, an Italian woman, adored Tony Bennett. She'd bought one of his albums in a used record store and fell in love with him and San Francisco.

Over and over she would play that song about the city by the bay. That smooth, velvety voice took her away from the filth of the "Garden State" she only knew. And transported her to that jewel of the West Coast with its hills, Fisherman's Wharf, and that magnificent engineering feat, the Golden Gate Bridge.

That album was her escape from a shitty marriage. Papa was a stout Polish man who died when I was only a kid. Too much beer and kielbasa led to a massive heart attack. It didn't help that my parents waited until their late thirties to have children. In my eyes, they were always "old."

Memories of Papa are limited to constant barking and belching. Belching and barking. Mostly at Mama, who could do nothing right. At one time, Mama said there was happiness when they dated, and he would take her to the movies, dance halls, and bring fresh flowers.

The grind of working at one of the last operating factories in town and hanging out at the bar afterwards became Papa's daily routine until we buried him and what he sadly thought was an inconsequential life when the undertaker closed the coffin lid on his body.

Mama raised my sibling and me in an Italian neighborhood in an old industrial city of North Jersey. Just short of my twenty-first birthday, she kicked me out of the house.

Smoking weed, drinking PBRs, gambling in the alley behind the little row house we called home, fighting, and never, ever backing down, I was a bad example for Cassandra, my baby sister. Mama was doing triage. Hoping to save one of the last of the Jankowski clan worth saving.

I adjust my tall frame against the piling of the pier I lean against in downtown Cedar's Point, a bustling town at the Jersey Shore. The Cormorant River it sits on flows to the bay, which connects to the Atlantic Ocean. Not too far away, tourists flock to iconic beach towns with their carnival-like boardwalks, greasy foods, and amusement rides.

My wavy jet-black hair blows in the June breeze. This is a good place to rest as I write in my tattered journal. A would-be writer, I keep this chronicle with the hope someday of getting published. English and lunch were the only subjects I did well in.

Creative writing became a passion, nurtured on by a

little old lady, Mrs. Schnitzer, who taught the subject with discipline but with love and encouragement. Somehow she looked beyond my dark soul and appearance and pushed me to write.

Red marks all over my papers were not meant to defeat. But to uplift. To take a dive within myself to do better. To use words to paint a picture. This teacher often told our class, we were artists...only with the pen and keyboard, instead of with a paintbrush.

Whatever shred of self-worth I have left, I owe it to Mrs. Schnitzer for sticking with me. May God rest her soul since she passed several years ago. What would she think about me using my talents as a diversion from this crappy existence? I wonder.

Are you surprised I can write? Me, a homeless "bum," as some callous and unfeeling people might say. Homeless people aren't dumb. Sadly, that's the stereotype.

We have the same dreams. The same innate intelligence. Life's circumstances— a bad divorce, bankruptcy, foreclosure, loss of employment, high medical bills, for example—can force folks to the streets, however. Don't forget that. Please.

I watch diners at the waterfront restaurant eat their seafood and pasta. Drink their craft beer and wine and toast the sun as it sets across the west. The colors reflect off the harbor, broken up only by the pleasure boats that come and go from the busy port.

With my large nose pushed in from too many brawls, I close my mouth and take a deep whiff of the salt air. Clean.

Without pollution. One of the few pleasures I have in life is sitting at this place before the winter comes.

How can I be homeless amid such huge wealth? I ask myself. How did it come to this that I'm a drifter at the Jersey Shore?

Over to my right, a bride and groom have photos taken. She's a beautiful redhead with freckles and a creamy complexion with two attendants trailing behind as they carry her long train.

The groom's muscled arms bulge against the material of his black and gray tuxedo. He has golden hair, topping off an aura that exudes he's a "golden boy." His longer locks and fit torso scream out—I'm an athlete and surfer.

I can see him over on the barrier island that protects the area from the power of the ocean. His wet suit keeps him warm. He rides the waves in triumph as the two-million-dollar homes with their multiple balconies, hot tubs, and incredible views provide a rich panorama. These manmade monstrosities join sand dunes, beach fencing, and lots of sunbathers whose only worries are putting enough sunscreen on and staying hydrated.

I wish this couple well, mumbling, "Hope it works out for ya better than it did with me and my girlfriend." A reason, not the only one though, for my current state.

Not too far away on their fancy condo deck, an elderly man and woman feed the seagulls. I've taken to naming these birds with each batch that swoops around me. "Frankie, Jane, Virgil, Carol." I have no idea if they're male or female.

A mix of black and white and gray—other than fighting over food—the gulls get along much better than the citizens of this society. Racial strife, income inequality, and sharp political differences have made for a less than perfect union, I note with irony.

Homelessness is the great equalizer. On the streets, we don't give a shit whether you're African American, Caucasian, gay, straight, transgender, Asian, male or female, legal or illegal. It's about survival. It's about the next meal, the next place to lay your head.

As crazy as it seems, giving the seagulls an identity is a way to pass time. For the homeless, time drags on. The clock stops. Life is in slow motion, torturous and cruel. Every step is a struggle. Every night pretty much sleepless and dark. Always dark. Always scary.

My attention shifts to the huge flag of freedom that anchors this area that serves as my temporary home. As a real smartass, I call it "the banner of opportunity." I mutter aloud, 'cause the moment calls for it, "Some opportunity if you have a prison record."

Don't get me wrong. I did bad things and did my time (more on that later) but I'm willing to work. I'm desperate to earn a living. That block on every job application: "Do you have a criminal record?" It's a killer when you mark "Yes." Lie and check "No," and your rap sheet eventually catches up to you.

CHAPTER TWO

"Hey, you can't sit there with all that junk," a young cop yells over from his bike, interrupting my musings. On patrol along the waterfront, keeping order, my appearance and stuff clash with his idea of what this pier should look like. The regular police rarely bother those of us who make this our daytime home during warm weather. Not this kid, only a few years younger than me.

"I'm not botherin' anyone," I say. The black and white book in front of me remains my determined focus as I shake my pen to keep the ink flowing. This instrument connects me to the paper and my thoughts.

And to my reality. Which I tell myself really sucks. If I think too hard and project beyond each day, the tears start. The lined journal and words are smudged and stained as evidence of all the water that has fallen from my eyes.

"Look, the town spent a lot of money to make this nice for residents and visitors. You don't fit in. And there's no loitering," he adds.

This is bullshit. How do you enforce that when there are lots of people walking around or sitting on benches to enjoy the view? I'm in no position to argue with this rent-a-cop, however.

"Okay, I'm leaving already," I answer. As I brush aside the long wisp of hair that covers my right eye, I stare hard at him. It's the first time we make real eye contact. My way of saying, *Yo, asshole. I know I haven't showered in days and my clothes are dirty and my appearance is shit against the backdrop of this summer wonderland. Can't a guy catch a break, though?*

The journal goes into my knapsack, a gift from one group that serves the homeless of the area. Stuffed full, I've got a flip cell phone, the only lifeline and connection I have to the greater world, cigarettes—you ask, how can he afford to smoke? Better than the pills and weed I used to do, I answer, beating you to your rushed judgment—two packs of crackers and granola bars, a flashlight, jeans, gym shorts, two extra shirts, a pair of socks and underwear, deodorant, toothpaste and toothbrush, toilet paper and baby wipes, and bottles of water—something I never have enough of.

Before I grab for the Army duffel bag that holds my sleeping bag, two blankets, a pillow, two small blue tarps, the thermal underwear I hold on to for the cold weather, a white sailboat, probably twenty feet or so, glides in toward the pier.

No longer under sail, it's powered by a small outboard motor and its captain and crew are three females. *No men on board and no competition in sight,* I note.

If I were my old confident self, I'd jump on the boat

and make a move. One woman waves and smiles. Petite with a copper glow and shoulder-length brunette hair with a brilliant sheen to it, she looks fantastic in a bright yellow bikini.

I do a double take as if to signal—*You're waving at me?* But I regain my composure and return the gesture, only not with quite as much gusto.

Despite being homeless, I'm not all that bad looking. Tall, dark, ruggedly handsome, I have broad shoulders, well-defined biceps, big hands, and strong hairy legs. With pale blue eyes (my Polish heritage coming through?), I still have all my teeth—not on the streets long enough to lose any. Yet.

Because shaving is a luxury I can't afford—why waste water and carry around shaving cream and a razor?—I have a full beard and a mustache with a tinge of red. My facial hair covers a deep cleft in my chin and dimples on my cheeks—marks, before I stopped shaving, that women loved about my looks.

She's still far enough away not to see how dirty my khaki shorts and a blue tee shirt are. Still, this encounter with "yellow bikini girl" provokes both lust and a twinge of dignity when I have very little of either. The homeless live in the shadows. It feels good to be noticed by someone pretty, with money to spend, as she motors around on a large sailboat.

The heavy duffel bag gets slung over my shoulder while I carry the knapsack. These are the entirety of my belongings. This is my personal wealth. This is my legacy in life. Should I die on the streets, this is the inheritance left behind. *Will anyone care*? I wonder.

Chapter Three

Several days have passed since I was chased away from the pier. That means several nights "sleeping" at my usual spot. My walk from the downtown to my nighttime home is about three miles. Since I'm in pretty good shape, it takes less than an hour to make it there. I hate the nights. It's the only time I'm really scared. I feel unprotected, vulnerable.

The spot I've chosen during the mild weather is in the woods off the Garden State Parkway, the major highway that connects North Jersey with the beaches of the Jersey Shore. I'm not sure whether I sleep (and trespass) on public or private lands. When I leave the area to trudge somewhere else, I scrub it clean. I don't want any evidence I've been there.

For two reasons really. One, if it's private land, I don't want to be discovered and driven off. Second, I don't want someone else who's homeless to claim it as their "own" where they get the idea from me that it's a decent place to set up. I hear there are "tent" sites of homeless scattered in other woods not too far away but I haven't ventured over there to check it out. Maybe in the winter.

There's a single concrete culvert sitting above ground, long since abandoned from an earlier project, that provides some extra protection when the heavy wind and rain comes. Next to the big pipe is a slight depression that allows me to put down one tarp, and the blankets and sleeping bag. I've laid down lots of pine needles to provide a little cushion.

Overhead, the other blue tarp is fashioned between the top of the culvert with a rope I use to tie it around, and two tall branches I use as poles. It's a crude, makeshift lean-to that provides cover from the elements. At some point, I know I'll need to secure a tent as the weather gets worse.

A fitful night's sleep doesn't come easily. When I hear a crackle of branches, I wake up. Is it someone who plans on attacking me? No, it's only a deer. The woods are plentiful with them.

Although I'm a fallen Catholic, I say a silent prayer each night before turning in. "God, please protect me tonight. Help me find a way out of being homeless. Amen." Out of habit, I make the sign of the cross and try to close my weary eyes.

Many nights, they refuse to cooperate. I look up into the blackness, broken up by the tiny specks of light. I feel even smaller and inconsequential as a result. And I wonder, in that moment of time, how many homeless people join me in gazing up into the big sky? How many of us are there who have no home to call our own? This is a club—sadly not too exclusive in America—nobody wants to belong to.

CHAPTER FOUR

Each morning, I clean up the site and walk to the convenience store not too far away. A small cup of coffee joins the granola bar reserved for breakfast. When I enter the corner shop, I leave my bundle outside the door. I worry about someone stealing it. Then what'll I do?

Before leaving, I go to the restroom. Thankfully my bowels are like clockwork, and this is the spot I use. I wash my hands good and brush my teeth from the toothbrush and toothpaste I pull out of my front pocket. I also fill two empty plastic water bottles.

With the hot coffee (something warm or steaming is always a luxury to savor), I sit against the building and light up a cigarette. Generic brands only are what I smoke. I try and limit myself to five a day. Or about a pack and half a week that eats up about fifteen dollars of my meager budget.

Where does the money come from? Odd jobs here and there and charity. Most folks don't hand out cash because of the fear it will be used for drugs and alcohol, but I have a staple of people who give me gift cards, including one of the food pantries I frequent. I'm grateful for this help.

There's a car wash that hires me to dry and detail automobiles. The money is under the table and I appreciate the owner letting me work for tips.

He's one of the few local employers who doesn't care about my criminal record. He made it clear to me, and I'm sure to others who towel off cars for him, "Take anything from a vehicle and I'll fire you on the spot and call the cops. Count on it." The last thing I need is an arrest and a return to prison.

After enjoying a cigarette—I'll worry about lung cancer later when I've got my life together—I stretch my twenty-three-year-old body. Try sleeping on the ground all the time. The body gets achy and stiff…regardless of how young I may be.

When I encounter my older homeless "friends" on the streets, I can't imagine how much they must hurt. I watch them shuffle around and realize that things could be worse.

Chapter Five

From Tony's Journal
June 27, 2015
Day 45 of Homelessness

It's a food pantry day. I walk the few miles to the local Methodist Church whose simple white clapboard and steeple contrasts with the ornate Catholic Church I remember from my youth. Instead of a crucifix, inside hangs a plain oak cross.

The pantry opens at nine o'clock and I arrive early. While there's plenty of food and toiletries, I worry, what if they run out? Then what? I find the usual pine tree that serves as my resting place until the church opens.

This part of the Jersey Shore sits at the edge of the "Pine Barrens," a large swath of Jersey with lots of pine and scrub trees. I love the fragrance of the evergreen almost as much as I love the salt air.

Unfortunately, I catch a whiff of my odor and it ruins the moment. There's only so much deodorant and baby wipes can do before the body stinks. Badly. My stench is a combination of what my old high school locker room smelled like with its wet moldy towels, stinky socks and jocks discarded on the floor, and foul toilets.

I haven't had a shower for two or three weeks. A small church team will drive to downtown once a month with their mobile van equipped with hot showers and a washer and dryer for the homeless to clean up and have laundry done. Like those working this food pantry, these people are angels of mercy.

Sitting by the tree gives me a chance to catch up on writing. For obvious reasons, I don't keep the journal at night and probably won't in the depths of winter when it's too fucking cold to hold a pen and write—unless I'm fortunate by then to escape the streets.

CHAPTER SIX

The doors open, the journal goes down, and I jump up to get in line. Some of the usual folks are waiting to receive their allotment, including people who are illegal. Again, I don't give a shit. The Mexican lady with three kids in tow needs as much help as I do. Maybe more. We're all hungry.

The pantry doesn't ask for ID. That would drive away those who live in the underground.

Occasionally, I'll pick up a newspaper left behind on a park bench. I scan it not only to read the news but to study how reporters write. If I want to be an author, I need to understand how others put words together, right? I read about the wall to keep illegals out.

With a cackle in her high-pitched voice, Mrs. Schnitzer said to stay away from politics and religion—she loved romance and mysteries—when we write unless we hoped to be reporters or politicians. I can't see myself in either of those jobs. So…I'll hold my opinion to myself.

Now that I'm at the front of the line, I enter the church. Mrs. Seidel, one of the Methodists who runs the pantry, greets me.

With a big smile, she says, "Hi, Tony. Wonderful to see you." She reaches to pull me into a hug over the white enamel counter that divides us. A touch with another human being is so rare, I hold our grasp for as long as she permits without it becoming creepy or sexual.

Mrs. Seidel is a kind, middle-aged woman. A little heavy in the hips and legs, her brown hair is graying. She has the purest eyes, framed with those retro "cat lady" glasses that seem to be back in style. I remember reading somewhere that a great author once said, "Eyes are the window to the soul."

Next time I'm at the big library downtown, I make a mental note to research the quote. I love this sanctuary of books as a writer and because I've been advised by the other homeless it'll be open in the winter as a place to pass time and stay warm. And perhaps catch up on my journal entries.

Mrs. Seidel has a good soul as I stare into her eyes. She doesn't look down on those of us needing this help.

During one of my first visits, she asks about my background. I tell her I want to be a writer. She shares with me that she retired from a county job and lost her husband about five years ago. She adds that the church and the food pantry are her reasons for existence.

"Thanks, Mrs. Seidel. God bless ya," I say. And I mean it. I couldn't make it without this help. She hands me the church's checklist and a pen to fill out what I need. I'm pretty good on toiletries right now so I leave those blank. Out of food for the most part, I check off granola bars, peanut butter and jelly, a box of dry cereal, water, cans of fruit and tuna fish, and a loaf of bread.

Along with the other food pantry I visit, I should get by for the week besides the little I buy at the convenience store. If there's money left on the gift cards or if I have a little extra cash, I sometimes treat myself to one of their pretzels. They're amazing.

I give her back the checklist and pen and the heavy-duty bag I use to carry food. With a touch of embarrassment—my face feels flush to prove it—I mention I need clean underwear and socks, knowing they keep a small supply of these items. What I have on is crunchy. This Methodist lady returns with all the things I asked for.

"Here you go, Tony." Before handing it over the counter, she drops in a five-dollar gift card to my favorite convenience store. It's like gold. "Thanks for coming, Tony. It's a blessing to serve you," she concludes.

I believe she means it. It's almost as if she has a rush of adrenaline because she's helping me and the others.

"Thanks, Mrs. Seidel. See ya next week. Make sure you thank everyone at the church," I add, since I know it takes a lot to run this pantry. I put a few things in the knapsack since it's easier to access. The food bag then goes in the duffel bag.

Before leaving, I ask if I may use the restroom. "You know where it is, Tony. Help yourself," Mrs. Seidel says.

I enter and lock the door and shed my clothes. With more baby wipes, I clean up and toss the old underwear and socks into a plastic bag and put on some new briefs.

I hope this helps with my smell. The worn stuff will get thrown out in the church's dumpster behind the building. After exiting the bathroom and a final smile from Mrs. Seidel, I move on.

CHAPTER SEVEN

There remains a line waiting to be served and the pantry will be open for at least two more hours to make sure everyone gets food. Again, I'm struck by the enormous need of those down and out as I gaze over at a development of mini-mansions that anchor this part of the neighborhood.

Their manicured lawns, large white columns that support upper balconies with views to die for of the lagoons that wind through the community, and four-car garages that house fancy automobiles and other play toys of the rich, stir a jealousy in me and the others in this food queue.

I think about last week when a black Cadillac pulled up and a man and woman get out to get free stuff. There was a buzz up and down the line. Everyone had the same reaction of: "Bullshit. These people don't need help. They're driving that car and their clothes are a lot cleaner than ours."

None of us try to hide our anger and resentment. Who the fuck are these assholes to get free food? Food reserved for *us*, the real poor.

When it's my turn that day, I say to Mrs. Seidel, "You're not gonna serve 'em, are ya? See that Caddy. They have a handicapped pass, too, and parked in that spot. They look like they're gettin' around pretty good." I point to these cheaters and the luxury automobile with an accusatory finger. My face is red-hot, and my fists are balled as I say this.

She's no dummy and answers with a smile. "This church doesn't judge, Tony. If someone abuses the help, that's between them and God. There might be circumstances we don't know about." Mrs. Seidel pats my arm to make sure I understand there's no sting to what she's saying and no rebuke against me for being angry.

The encounter—and these volunteers for the Lord—prompts me to think about Christian love and all that training I received as a child growing up in the Catholic Church. That's one thing Mama insisted on: attending Mass and confession. Which I did until my later teen years…when I rebelled against the Church and Mama.

These people are trying to reflect God's love, I say to myself. They don't preach at us. They feed us. And they love us. I remember Jesus doing the same from my religious education and ponder what all this means as I sit down at the same evergreen tree to write some more and have lunch before moving on to the next stop.

CHAPTER EIGHT

From Tony's Journal
July 5, 2015
Day 53 of Homelessness

Last night, I joined several thousand other people to watch the fireworks over the harbor. Happy Fourth, America. With such a huge crowd, I felt like I blended in. It helped that I left the duffel bag and knapsack behind at the campsite. Risky but worth it to celebrate the holiday as a "normal" person. Without these items, the trek in seems so much easier, too.

While the pyrotechnics burst and fell over the smooth water, I allowed myself to be a kid again although I have no memory of Mama and Papa ever taking us to a firework display back in the 'hood.

Around the streets we'd run with sparklers instead and my buddies and I would light and toss firecrackers at the girls, who we were trying to impress. They'd squeal and sometimes we'd get lucky and kiss them in the darkness of the alleys and hidden corners of old, abandoned warehouses. These locations later would become the pre-ferred place for more advanced sexual exploration.

Earlier today, the mobile mission showed up at the downtown church that plays hosts to this vehicle where we can wash up. When my turn came, I entered and shucked off my soiled clothes. Limited to a five-minute shower, I don't complain.

I luxuriate in the hot water and lather my body as if I'm staying in a five-star hotel where the spa attendant will hand me a soft terrycloth robe as I exit. Every part of my body scrubbed with abandonment, I wash my thick hair and squeeze out the accumulated grease and grime.

After rinsing and drying off with the fluffy towel the volunteer provided, I put on jeans and a shirt. The same person takes my dirty clothes and he bags them and gives me a "receipt," understanding how important the few possessions I have are to me. The mission will launder the clothes and I'll return after writing to pick up my clean bundle.

Nestled in an alcove of the church that abuts the parking lot they share with other businesses, it's a good spot to think and the cops won't bother me here.

I'm sort of blathering on because I want to avoid as long as possible the obvious question. How did I become homeless? What went wrong? Lots of things, really. So, here goes…

Chapter Nine

Back to the day when Mama kicked me out. Another day doing absolutely nothing. Hungover, laying on the living room sofa, a joint in one hand, controller in the other. A beer on the end table within easy reach. Other than a part-time job as a short-order cook and busboy at the local diner, I didn't do shit each day.

Video games, getting high, fighting and gambling. This was my life.

Mama came down the steps with her black dress on. She hadn't worn it since Papa died. This was the lead up and signal she meant business. I was so clueless that I kept playing the electronic game. Thankfully, Cassandra was at school and didn't see this scene.

"Put that thing down now," Mama says.

"After I finish this game," I answer, intent on killing the bad dude running across the screen. Oblivious, right? Living only in the moment.

"Now, Anthony. We're gonna talk," she says in broken English even though Mama's lived in America for most of her life. With narrowed brown eyes, she's pointing her index finger my way.

"Okay, already. Chill, Mama." I only make her angrier with my lousy attitude.

"Here's a money for bus fare…to get you started until you find a job." She hands me an envelope. Mama's pupils gaze into mine. There are no tears or sadness. Only determination.

"Where am I goin'? What'd I do? I have a job." I say.

"Son, you know what you did. You're a bad example for Cassandra. I want you outta this house. Your cousin Angelo…he's agreed to take you in."

Angelo comes from my mother's side; we'd met a few times at family weddings and funerals. A few years older than me, I knew he lived somewhere at the Jersey Shore.

"I'm not goin' anywhere. Not to Angelo's and the Jersey Shore. This is my home. I'll change. Tell me what I gotta do." I'm trying to negotiate with someone who is done negotiating. "We've been over this before, Anthony. Such a bad boy," Mama shakes her head, looks to heaven, and makes the sign of the cross. "Pack your things and get outta. The bus leaves in one hour."

Mama turns and heads back up the narrow wood steps. I notice a slight slouch to her shoulders and body. For the first time, I also spot the rosary in her fist. She'd been praying for the courage to toss me out.

All my life, I've struggled to control my temper. This moment was no different and I knock over the mahogany two-tiered end table next to the sofa. The large garish lamp that Mama prizes breaks and my beer spills all over the worn brown carpet.

Mama comes back down the steps. Now I've really pissed her off. "Any more fits, Anthony, and I call the *polizia*." Anytime Mama breaks into Italian is an indication her patience is over.

She adds, "This is *my home, not yours*." I give her one last look of resistance and realize this is no false alarm. I follow her up the steps to my little room, where I slam the door shut to maintain the semblance of some dignity during this eviction.

Reluctantly, I pull out from under the twin bed an Army duffel bag that'd belonged to Papa, who had served in the military before marrying Mama. Stamped with his name and rank, "Jankowski, Stanley R. Sergeant," I fill it with clothes from the old cherry dresser my grandmother passed down. Tears now run down my cheeks and I try to breathe in between sobs.

CHAPTER TEN

Twenty years old and all I know is over. Mama's in her bedroom and she's turned on the record player and the Tony Bennett album. The record skips from all the times she's played it. Once again, she's escaping and doesn't want to hear my reaction to this momentous decision of hers.

After finishing up with the dresser and duffel bag and throwing toiletries in, I open the envelope. There's a bus ticket to Cedar's Point, Angelo's town, his address and phone number are scrawled in Mama's tiny handwriting on a small card, and three hundred dollars in cash. I feel no guilt even though this represents much of what Mama has saved.

Money is always, always tight. She won't have another mouth to feed and can focus all her attention on Cassandra. From her viewpoint, this is a worthwhile investment. In my wallet, I have about forty dollars to add to what's in the envelope.

Back down the steps, before opening the solid front door with a peephole—we don't live in the best neighborhood—I pick up the end table and drop my house key on it. The hell with cleaning up the spilled beer and broken ceramic pieces that's all that remains of the lamp. *She can do it,* I say to myself. I notice my joint has a little glow left to it and ground it out on the arm of the sofa to leave my last mark within the Jankowski household.

I take one more look around the drab living room that leads to a small dining room with its walnut depression table and black gothic chairs where I don't remember any happy family meals. Only sadness and anger ruled over this room.

Behind the dining room sits a tiny kitchen dominated by a stove and olive-green refrigerator from the sixties (also left behind by my grandmother). Soiled wallpaper with gaudy hearts and polka dots looks back at me from these rooms.

Although it's worn, cramped, and hasn't been spruced up during my entire life here, it's still home. It's all I've ever known. I open the door and leave.

The walk to the bus station is a short one. I pass the flower shop and dry cleaners. The only businesses on the street. Mrs. Ortenzio, the owner, is out front, taking a break from arranging flowers. Her focus now is sweeping the sidewalk that won't ever be clean no matter how hard she sweeps. And this determined little lady can sweep.

Despite the warm spring weather, she wears a shawl over her faded white dress that once had vibrant roses bursting forth to help advertise this shop. With gray hair tied off with a cloth scarf that proudly displays the Italian boot, her native land, she doesn't gaze up at me. Mrs.

Ortenzio knows me as a thug and a problem for Mama, her dear friend.

I mutter, "Never liked this 'hood, anyway." The tears have dried and I've shifted to defiance. Two city trash cans, always overflowing with garbage, frame her store. I kick the one can hard and startle Mrs. Ortenzio.

She hisses at me, "*Feccia*." Not the first time she's called me this, it means "scum." I give her a wicked grin and the finger. Mrs. Ortenzio spits on the sidewalk; the wad of saliva her final goodbye to nothing but trouble.

At the bus station, I'm greeted by a homeless man at the entrance, who begs me for a dollar, so he can buy a cup of coffee. Hunched over, he sits on the hard ground. Several large trash bags stuffed full of his possessions surround him. A long, gray beard, red wool hat pulled over his head in sixty-five-degree weather, and dirty crimson sweatshirt and gray sweats, remind me of a poor Kris Kringle.

Without a shred of compassion, I answer, "Get a job, old man."

Instead of cursing me, he says with a sparkle in his blue eyes, "God bless ya, young man. Have a good day."

Little did I realize then that my time would come on the streets. The big guy in the sky has a way of squaring things away. And, in my case, causing a major attitude readjustment to come as homelessness morphs me from a no-good hoodlum into a sensitive, caring, mature young man.

CHAPTER ELEVEN

From Tony's Journal
August 10, 2015
Day 89 of Homelessness

Like the homeowner who ignores the drip, drip, drip of the kitchen faucet and refuses to call a plumber, I continue to avoid the entire back story on how I became homeless. Sorry I'm not putting it out there all at once. Be patient, please.

Drifting through much of the summer in the same routine, I look forward to those days when I'm fortunate enough to work at the car wash.

The dog days of August, Cedar's Point is suffering through a heat wave along with the rest of the East Coast. Extreme temperatures and humidity make it very difficult to sleep—I obviously have no air conditioning—and I fill up water bottles wherever I can: the convenience store, library, gas stations, churches.

Today is a car wash day. The call came yesterday to show up for work. Here I am at eight o'clock, ready for the operation to open at nine. I hope to pick up at least thirty dollars in tips during this shift. Saving for a tent, winter will dramatically shift my living circumstances and tarps won't be enough. I can't be out in the woods completely exposed to the elements.

So…back to how I ended up living in the woods.

CHAPTER TWELVE

After getting on the bus I arrived at the station in Cedar's Point. Angelo wasn't there to meet me. I can't say I blame him, though. He didn't ask for this assignment and we really didn't know each other well despite being first cousins.

I took a cab over to his place, an apartment in a large Victorian converted into four or five apartments. On the second floor, Angelo's apartment is accessible from an old iron staircase at the rear of the property.

First impression: this stop in my life isn't much of a promotion from the family homestead. "Beggars can't be choosers," however. I ignore the beat-up metal trash cans, rusted chain-link fence, and three cars—all vintage from the late eighties or early nineties and all patched up. One Chevy's front end is smashed in and it looks like the owner has no intention of having it repaired.

Up the steps I go, I find Angelo's door and knock. No answer. I bang harder then and wait. *Maybe he's at work*, I say to myself. Another five minutes pass and I bang again.

Cousin Angelo finally comes to the door and flings it open, cursing. Angelo's in white boxer shorts and nothing else. Like me, his hair is ink-black, only slicked back with lots of gel product used to give him this greasy look. Same big nose and wide mouth. Of medium height, Angelo needs to visit the gym more. Kind of flabby, a lot of dark fuzz covers his chest and belly.

On the sofa behind him, I guess, sits his girlfriend. She's dressed in an extra-large green tee shirt that reaches to her knees. Probably one of his, it reads "Billy's Auto Shop." I remember hearing Angelo's a car mechanic.

The girlfriend's scowling from the interruption. With highlights to her brown hair—done in a pixie cut with shaved sides—she wears no makeup, giving her a rather severe look. The only pop of real color comes from her toenails and fingernails, painted bright red.

"Dude, you're timing fuckin' sucks," Angelo says. "Kinda in the middle of something."

"Sorry, bro, I can come back. Is there a place to grab a burger?" I say.

Angelo's closing the door as he answers, "Around the corner."

There's a diner nearby and the waitress brings me a hamburger, French fries, and a strawberry milkshake. With money plentiful at that point, I didn't pause from ordering an expensive shake. I have no idea if Angelo plans on charging me rent. Find a job and crash at his place as long as possible are my immediate goals.

Chapter Thirteen

After about an hour, I go back to his apartment. I knock again, and Angelo opens right away. In jeans and a tee shirt, there is no sign of his girlfriend whose name I learn is "Belinda."

"C'mon in, cousin. Belinda and I finished up. You know how it is," he says with a punch to my arm after we shake hands.

"Yeah, sorta. I had no real privacy at Mama's. She had this way of walkin' into my bedroom at the wrong time," I answer, remembering several times when I scrambled to cover up my girlfriend and me with a blanket so at least Mama didn't see us naked. These moments would cause her to curse in Italian and she'd cross herself after exiting quickly.

"Well, listen, Tony, you can stay here…at least for a little while. The place is small, and I'm not supposed to have more than one person here. Don't need any shit from the landlord. C'mon for a quick tour," he gestures.

We go into the small living room papered with posters of Superman, a boxer flexing his biceps next to a topless model holding his championship belt, Han Solo of *Star Wars* fame, and the rock band Kiss.

"You'll sleep on the sofa," he points to where Belinda was sitting, and I suspect where they "finished up," as my cousin said. The upholstery at one time might've been white. It's now covered with stains from food, drinks, cigarette ash, and whatever else left behind from their lovemaking.

Angelo lights up a cigarette. Probably his second one after sex. "Smoke?" he says, offering me one from the pack.

"Not cigarettes, just weed," I say. Tobacco comes later.

"Not in here, bro. Belinda's a recovering addict. Can't have her around that shit." I nod my head, knowing I'll have to find another spot to get high.

Off the living room, the tiny kitchen is loaded with dirty dishes in the sink, a plastic trash can with all kinds of garbage overflowing around it, a stack of empty pizza boxes leans up against a rust-colored stove covered with at least an inch of stinky grease, and a 1940s style refrigerator is wedged in between the stove and the old white enamel sink.

Angelo opens the frig door and pulls out a beer. "Want one?" he says.

"Sure." I twist off the cap and watch Angelo flick his across the space towards the garbage can. He misses and lets it join the rest of the mess on the floor. Mine gets placed into a mayo jar that's perched at the top of the pile.

I don't wanna get too comfortable here, I say to my-self, as I take a deep pull from the brown bottle. It's an off-brand lager and I can't help but make a face when it hits my taste buds.

We leave the kitchen and Angelo points inside his little bedroom. Piled full of his clothes: socks, underwear, shorts, several pairs of his work coveralls, lay all over the wood floor and his black dresser.

The bed's unmade and now I know why Belinda likes the sofa. He has no sheets. Only a thin New York Giants blanket "lays" on top of the bare mattress.

"Sorry for the mess, Tony. I work so much…the place is what it is."

We end up in the bathroom and now I understand why Mama sent me here. Somehow she knew this was a sentence to Hell.

There are several dozen empty toilet paper rolls on the worn vinyl floor along with old razors, soap wrappers, and shampoo bottles with little liquid left, and more underwear and socks. *Doesn't this guy put anything away. I'm not exactly "Mister Clean" but there's probably a virus growing in here or something.*

With no cleaning products in sight, the toilet, sink, and shower are filthy. There are more black spots—likely mold?—than the original white. Judging by the area around the bowl, Angelo sucks at hitting the water, and should have a sign posted as a reminder to watch how he aims his firehose.

While we're standing there, Angelo decides he has to go as he unbuttons his jeans. I look away briefly to avoid seeing my cousin's penis, and then look back as he's zipping up. He proves my point as I notice only some of his piss made it into the porcelain bowl.

After a large belch, he sighs, "That feels better." He does not flush, content to leave the toilet yellow.

"Make yourself at home," he says as he runs his hands under the water. There's no hand towel nearby and he shakes the excess water onto the floor as we exit. Note to self: *Pick up flip flops to wear around this shithole before something grows on my feet.*

"Stow your shit away in the corner of the living room. Probably should buy a sheet and pillow for the sofa, cousin, since Belinda and I use it. I don't have any extras," he adds. *Or any,* I want to say, but I keep my mouth shut.

Back out in the living room, I sit down on my new "bed." Angelo joins me and hands over a video controller hooked up to a box and flat screen television. "I only have one rule, dude. When I hang a sock on the front door knob, it means me and Belinda are busy. You'll have to come back later."

I nod. To be polite I swallow more of the bad tasting beer as I take another look around my new home. A place to crash, and that's it. Cousin Angelo says nothing about rent and I don't offer to pay any.

He doesn't ask about what prompted Mama to throw me out and I'm thankful for that. Guys usually understand some things are better left unsaid.

We settle into playing games. Two cousins with little in common other than our mothers are sisters from the old country.

CHAPTER FOURTEEN

From Tony's Journal
August 11, 2015
Day 90 of Homelessness

A full work day at the car wash brought ninety dollars in tips. Great, financially. But not so much for my self-esteem, which got knocked around pretty good. Other than fellow travelers on the streets and the folks working in the food pantries, Cousin Angelo and Belinda, and my ex-girlfriend Dawn, I am anonymous as I go about my business. Not yesterday, however.

The day was almost over. Soaked between the humidity and being around the high-pressure industrial sprayers that wash and rinse the cars as they pass through, the last car comes down the line. A four-door champagne-colored Lexus convertible—fully loaded and low in mileage—it's very clean inside but I still vacuum and dry the car as if it had come out of a junkyard. That's what the boss expects, and I don't want to lose my only job.

I had a break before this vehicle and counted forty bucks in tips. Enough to buy cigarettes, more minutes for the flip phone, and perhaps get the tent if I can find a cheap one with what I've already saved.

CHAPTER FIFTEEN

As I finish up on the luxury auto, the owner comes towards me. I pull my Jersey Devils ball cap down over my face to avoid this person. Too late, he's figured out my identity. A friend from grade school, this is the last guy I expected or wanted to see.

Blond, blue-eyed, tall, Brad was the "jock," the captain of the football team with all the cheerleaders trailing behind him in the hallways.

Me? I was the burnout, smoking pot, getting in brawls, the "bad boy" in high school.

Brad and I had been close in elementary school. He was the only non-Italian in the neighborhood and for some odd reason we'd bonded.

Basketball in the alley, cops and robbers in the nearby creek basin—he was the cop, I was the robber—catching a glimpse together of our first Playboy, stolen from Brad's older brother's bedroom, with neither of us understanding what the heck we were looking at other than viewing the pictures made us feel grown up.

When we grew up, we ignored each other in high

school. As our personalities formed—Brad's helped along by an intact family and incredible good looks, mine by being raised by a single mother with little supervision—Brad was popular, and classmates feared me because of my dark persona. That fear didn't translate to respect, however, other than from Mrs. Schnitzer.

Before this encounter at the car wash, I remember our last conversation at graduation. An awkward goodbye between two guys who had been buds when we were younger but who no longer had anything in common.

The exchange went something like this as we stood there in the ridiculous black robes with diplomas in hand.

"Well, good luck, Tony," he says.

"Yeah, you, too, Brad," I say.

"Where you off to? I'm heading to Brown."

Of course, you're goin' to an Ivy League university, I say to myself. But answer instead, "Community college or tech. I wanna be a writer, though. Still figurin' it all out."

Stamp my forehead with LIAR, LIAR, LIAR for spouting such bullshit. The only place I was destined for after graduation was the diner and a part-time job. We shook hands and I thought I'd never see him again. Until yesterday happened.

CHAPTER SIXTEEN

"Is that you, Tony?" he says.

I push the cap back up over my face and answer, "Yo, Brad, yeah, it's me." We grip and grin and I have a small victory my strength tops his through this ritual greeting. One measure of manhood.

Brad's dressed in a green polo shirt, pleated khaki pants, bright purple socks—his signature statement?—and expensive leather shoes. He reeks of wealth and I envy the way he glides effortlessly toward me. Very easy, very comfortable, very self-assured.

In my beat-up gym shorts and ratty black *Iron Maiden* tee shirt—I was into heavy metal back in the day; Brad, more of a *Green Day* fan—I reserve for car wash days, I'm wearing the same type of black Converse sneakers I wore in high school. Brad's moved up. I've moved down.

"What the hell are ya doing here, Tony? Is this your business?"

He can't be that clueless, so it must be his way of trying to ease my embarrassment. "Nah, this is one of my jobs. I work at an upscale restaurant over on the island.

Chef's assistant." More lies peddled to him as I spin a story of Tony Jankowski, "the success story." "How 'bout you? Looks like you're doin' pretty good."

"Wall Street, buddy, in a boutique firm. Lots of action there." *What the hell is that?* I wanna ask, but my goal is to end this conversation as soon as possible so I nod as if I understand the differences in financial organizations and the folks they cater to.

"The firm specializes in serving clients with at least a million dollars in liquid assets. I have a vacation home nearby...a condo on the waterfront. Maybe you can come over sometime for a cold one. Terrific view of the harbor and river from my balcony and a relaxing place to unwind away from the pressures of Manhattan. On a clear day, the bridge to the island is visible," he says.

"Sure, Brad, that'd be great. My apartment's outside of town. One of those old factories turned into lofts. Really cool industrial vibe. To be honest, I don't bother much with downtown. I'm more of an island guy."

God is gonna strike you dead for how much bullshit you're spewing, Tony, flashes through my mind. I don't tell him that having a brew would violate my sobriety. Earned courtesy of my time in prison. The less said, the better.

"How's your mom and Cassandra doing?"

The torture continues. "They're great. Really great. Couple times a summer they come down to hang out on the beach with me. How's your family?" I say.

"Doing well. Say hi to 'em for me. Thanks for the great job on the car, Tony." As we shake hands again, Brad puts a fifty-spot in my hand. Both grateful and seething, I haven't fought in quite some time but would love to punch him in the mouth. Those perfect white teeth broken by the force of my big fist.

"Thanks, Brad. Take care of yourself," I say instead.

Back inside to check in with my boss before leaving, one of my co-workers sees the exchange and asks about the big tip. "How 'bout a piece of that fat one, buddy?"

"Fuck off, man. You didn't help with his car." As deep as the humiliation goes to my core, I need the money.

I gather my things to head "home" to the woods and watch Brad pull out into traffic as he navigates the Lexus—with the top now down—back to his luxury place to grill a juicy Porterhouse steak and sip on expensive red wine while I make a peanut butter and jelly, capped off with a can of mixed fruit heavy with syrup.

CHAPTER SEVENTEEN

From Tony's Journal
August 21, 2015
Day 100 of Homelessness

I'm "celebrating" the milestone of one hundred days on the streets. Not from the campsite, harbor, car wash, or one of the food pantries, but from a hospital bed. Recovering from a head injury and bruised ribs, I've been in Cedar's Point Memorial for several days now.

Other than the almost constant headache, still being woozy, suffering from low blood pressure, and some dehydration from when I got here, it's kind of been like a hotel stay. Clean sheets and a comfortable mattress with three meals a day, the nurse's aide assisted me with a hot shower this morning.

George, my roommate, is loud and coarse. In his late fifties, his situation is far worse than mine and I've added a little prayer for him at nighttime. Like a soldier who finds religion in the foxhole, I've found myself drawn closer to God. Only I'm not in a military battle but a fight for survival in the America of the twenty-first century.

Overweight, diabetic, and on dialysis, George is legally blind. All his conversations carry through our room and into the hallway, and I gather he's a regular here. The health care workers have no patience left for my roomie; he is demanding, and his demeanor forces me to be extra polite when the nurses break away from George to care for me.

After breakfast, George had to go to the bathroom, and hospital staff have not cleared him to leave the bed to use the toilet. The orderly, a strong African American man in his late twenties, offered to bring a bedpan. George refused, insisting he wanted to "walk" to the facility we share, only a few steps from his bed. With George's condition, however, it's more like a mile to him and to those who basically must carry his big bulk there.

A contest of wills ensued with George yelling at the top of his lungs, "I'll shit right here unless you take me to the commode." The poor guy kicked the situation to the nursing supervisor and soon George was victorious, aided by the orderly and a sturdy nurse to make the "long trip."

I feel sorry for him. No one visits George—not that I have a royal court feting me or anything, but I hope to have a long life ahead and possess a fierce determination to end this homelessness. George is looking in the rearview mirror and is unlikely to leave his infirmities behind.

How did I get here? I remember little. The cops have filled in the blanks with some details and I've provided the facts on what happened before the attack occurred that landed me here.

Chapter Eighteen

Just another day. Or so I thought. After leaving the convenience store for my morning visit, I retraced my steps back to the campsite. At the edge of the parking lot, as I entered the woods, a "wolf pack" of teenagers confronted me, demanding my money.

As a big guy, I don't intimidate easily after all the fights in high school and on the streets of my native city. This time, however, the thugs outnumbered me.

Led by a juvenile as tall and strong in appearance as me, his dirty blond hair tied off in a man bun, he had drawn a black hunting knife with a serrated edge. Three other guys stood behind me and the parking lot to make sure I didn't run for it.

With their leader: a teenage girl whose flaming red curls could not hide a mouth fouler than anything I could ever say…and I've said my share of curse words. In her right hand, a baseball bat. From how she leaned into the wolf pack boss, I judged she was his girlfriend and the "brains" of the operation.

When I refused to give up my cash, "Man Bun" dude

lunged with the knife. The blade missed but I landed a blow to his chest with my strong fist.

But "Red," as I've come to call her, hit me on the right side of my skull with that wood bat stamped with some Major Leaguer's name on it. Somewhere under my thick hair, I have this baseball hero's signature imprinted on my head as "evidence" of the crime. With far more strength than her thin body looked capable of producing, down I went in what seemed like slow motion. After being knocked unconscious, apparently the group took turns kicking my torso.

The only thing they took from my possessions was the flashlight. Thankfully, my life savings was in my left shoe; where I keep money for just this reason since those who are homeless tend to be the subject of these kinds of violent attacks.

Chapter Nineteen

On the day of discharge, a social worker from the hospital visits. With thick brunette hair held straight back with a barrette, she has a kind face, framed with big green eyes that convey compassion and concern for the people she's serving.

In a strange way, she reminds me of a younger Mrs. Schnitzer. Maybe because I'm just not used to kindness coming my way—other than by the folks at the churches, like Mrs. Seidel, who treat the homeless as human beings.

In her hands is a clipboard with lots of papers and I spot "Anthony B. Jankowski" typed on many. She begins, "Mr. Jankowski, I'm Tina, the social worker for Cedar's Point Memorial. May I call you, Tony?"

"Sure, that'd be fine," I say.

"Before the hospital discharges you, Tony, we need to talk about where you're staying and how we can help with at least your medical situation."

Tina pauses as she glances over to my "stuff" that sits in the corner of the room. Fortunately, the police and ambulance crew made sure they transported my things to the hospital and I don't have to worry about starting completely over.

"From my bundle, Tina, you know I'm homeless and don't have health insurance. I can't pay the bill by the way," I add. When I was conscious enough to go over paperwork, I produced ID that showed my last address when I lived with my ex-girlfriend and stressed I had no medical coverage.

"We know, Tony, and don't expect you to," she says. "Medicaid is going to cover you from now on. The hospital staff will work with the state on the bill and any follow up you may need because of your injuries. We also have charitable care. Do you have a place you can stay until your body heals completely? It concerns the staff that you may be returning to your previous living arrangement." Tina knows I live in the woods or on the streets but can't bring herself to say the obvious.

"Angelo, my cousin, lives here in town. I bunked with him for a while before moving in with a girlfriend and that ended, too, before I went to prison. Angelo might lemme crash there for a few days before I return to my campsite," I say.

"What's his number, Tony? I'd be glad to call him. Make sure I give you the number, too, for someone who can help with housing."

"That'd be great if you'd call Angelo. Hearing from somebody else other than me is probably better. The housing advocates have tried to help before. The waiting lists are like really long, and there's little saved for a security deposit and rent. What I have is to pay for a tent to prepare for winter," I say. "Appreciate your help," I add, since this lady is trying.

My wallet is on the bedside table close to my cell phone. Somehow I was coherent enough at the emergency room to transfer my cash from my shoe to the wallet and I've been keeping it close by ever since.

From the fake leather billfold, I pull Angelo's number from a piece of scrap paper and hand it to Tina. Since I didn't live with him for very long, I never entered his information in the "contacts" in the flip phone.

Tina takes the information and dials Angelo's number, using the hospital phone that also sits on the bedside table. On the third or fourth ring, he answers. His voice carries through the receiver so I'm able to listen to both ends of the conversation.

"This is Angelo," he says.

"Angelo, this is Tina, a social worker at Cedar's Point Memorial. Tony, your cousin, is with me and is being discharged from the hospital today." "Yeah, what's that gotta do with me? Tony hasn't lived here in over two years. I'm busy and have to get to the shop."

"Your cousin's recovering from a head injury and bruised ribs and is in no condition to return to the place where he lives. Can he stay with you for a few days until he heals more?" she says.

There's a long pause before he answers. Belinda is in the background, yelling that she doesn't want me back. Angelo tells her to shut up. "Listen, I have a very small apartment and things didn't work out the last time Tony was here. Sorta walked in on me and my girlfriend one too many times. What the hell happened to him that he's hospitalized?" Angelo says. I can hear a small sliver of concern and I have some hope.

"A group attacked Tony behind the convenience store on Wake Street, looking for money. It's been a problem lately with the homeless, who are vulnerable to robbery and assault. They hit him with a baseball bat, pulled a knife, and busted his ribs.

"The police found Tony in the woods near the edge of the parking lot and he's been under our care for several days. I can't emphasize enough that Tony is not ready to return to his previous living space. If you can't help, are there other family members who can?" Tina says.

"Tony's mom won't have anything to do with him. He can stay here for two nights and that's it. Tell him the key will be in the old spot. Now I've gotta get to work. 'Bye." Angelo hangs up before Tina can say anything else.

"I heard. Thanks, Tina," I say.

"You're welcome, Tony. Just glad you have a place to sleep for at least a few days. Follow up with the doctors in a week and please call the housing folks again. Don't give up trying." Tina touches my arm as a gesture of kindness and has me sign lots of papers. I thank her again and she leaves.

CHAPTER TWENTY

The hospital provides one last hot meal, lunch, before I'm discharged. Meat loaf and mashed potatoes smothered in gravy, string beans, topped off with a chilled pineapple cup and ice-cold milk. I finish everything, leaving the plate clean. When you're homeless, one tends to eat like it may be your last meal.

Sam, the orderly my roommate abused, comes with a wheelchair to take me downstairs. In a louder voice, he says, "You've been a great patient, Tony." He's talking to me and George when he says this.

I get in the chair and Sam picks up my things and puts the knapsack on my lap with the discharge paperwork and the heavy Army duffel bag's strap slides easily over his strong shoulder as he pushes the transport toward the door. I ask him to stop at George's bed, so I can say goodbye.

With a gentle pat to his foot covered by the hospital sheet, I say, "Take care of yourself, George." To pass time, we had many conversations in which he shared with me the failures of two marriages, estrangement from his kids, and how not taking care of his body caused his serious medical condition. In a fatherly way, George encouraged me to keep fighting to get off the streets.

"Yeah, you, too, kid. You've been a good roommate. Sorry I lost it over using the bathroom. These hospital people treat us like barnyard animals." George's temporary softness ends as he glares in the direction of Sam's movements. Sam looks away, shaking his head in disgust.

"Don't sweat the small shit, George," I put my hand out to shake his, guiding his hand into my mine since he doesn't see too well. With a laugh I add, "Sam and the nurses are good peeps. Don't ride 'em too hard." He grunts, and Sam pushes me out into the hallway.

"Thanks for sticking up for us, Tony," Sam says. "That's one tough patient."

We enter the elevator and go down to the lobby. People are bustling about as Sam pilots me through the busy atrium. The automatic doors open, and Sam stops at a bench that sits just outside the overhang that protects the hospital entrance.

"Drop me here, Sam. Gonna call a cab to take me to my cousin's."

Reluctant to leave, he flashes me a look of concern. Sam knows I'm homeless and still healing.

"Thanks, man. I'll be okay," I assure him.

"Feel better, Tony, and stay safe." After shaking hands, I get up and sit on the bench and Sam places the duffel bag on the ground next to me. I watch him return inside and sadness overtakes me. The hospital was a place of safety and security. A temporary sanctuary away from the streets.

Prevented from smoking during my stay, I pull out a cigarette, light it up, and take a deep drag as I think about the coming time with Angelo. Round two with my cousin coming up.

CHAPTER TWENTY-ONE

From Tony's Journal
August 22, 2015
Day 101 of Homelessness

A faded green foreign compact—whose roof line was much too low for me and the tall driver as we both craned our necks down within the interior—was my ride over to Angelo's place from the hospital. About a fifteen-minute trip.

The talkative cab operator helped distract me from the almost nonstop anxiety I had at how this stay would go. With a nose more prominent than mine and big ears with lots of tangled jungle growing from his lobes, his hair is prematurely gray and in tight curls.

From Brooklyn, David is proud of his Jewish heritage and moved down to the Jersey Shore last year to escape the city and its high costs. Driving a cab is his second job, he explains. The first one is as a part-time custodian in the synagogue where he worships.

Since I'm becoming more and more interested in religion and finding God in the middle of this miserable existence, I pepper him with lots of questions about what it means to be Jewish. David explains the basics and says with a laugh, "If you ever wanna convert, kid, look me up."

At the front of Angelo's apartment building, I pull my wallet from my jean's pocket. David waves off the attempt at paying. "This one's on me, Tony. After what you've been through, I ain't taking your money. Stay outta trouble," he tells me.

I thank him and resolve moving forward to focus on the compassionate deeds done for me rather than the ridicule and violence that also has come my way during this difficult journey.

As Angelo promised, the key was in the old spot. I enter and notice not much has changed other than there's a newer sofa and recliner and several more posters on the wall. The flat screen television is larger than the one when I lived with him. No upgrades to the kitchen, his bedroom, or the bathroom.

Still piles of clothes and trash all over. Where the fuck is Angelo putting his money? I wonder. Other than spending it on Belinda and eating lots of pizza and take out, his life remains a constant of work and hanging in his disgusting apartment with his disgusting girlfriend.

After a quick shower, where I keep my flip flops on because Angelo still hasn't cleaned the tub, I pull my sleeping bag out of the duffel bag and lay it out on the couch, hoping to take a nap until Angelo comes home. With a head that feels like it has been in a vice, I grab for a pill, drinking from my water bottle rather than using one of Angelo's glasses from the sink.

CHAPTER TWENTY-TWO

Homecoming to the apartment wasn't a scene from the tear jerker Christmas movies from days gone by. Angelo kicks the sofa hard and I wake up with a jolt. Belinda is standing behind him with her hands on her hips, clothed only in tiny jean cut off shorts and a pink tee shirt that boldly reads "Jersey girls don't pump gas." If her eyes had been capable of shooting fire, I'd have been zapped dead.

"You look like shit, dude," he says. She just scowls. No greeting or attempt at compassion even though she knows I was beaten badly.

"Thanks for letting me stay here, Angelo," I say while rubbing my eyes. First instinct was to yell at this asshole move of his, but I hold my tongue and diplomacy prevails. "I won't get in the way," I promise, given the history we have.

"Two days, Tony. That's it. Belinda is not happy about this," he says.

She has moved to the bedroom and slammed the door shut to emphasize Angelo's point that if she had her way, I'd have recovered anywhere but that apartment.

"Here's ten bucks. Go grab yourself something to eat at the diner. We need privacy."

I know what this means. The reason I got booted originally was because I violated the "sock on the door knob" rule. Back then, I had to take a piss bad and walked in on my cousin in the middle of "lovemaking" with Belinda.

Why didn't I find somewhere else to urinate? The answer is I became comfortable after living with him for two months. And that's when Angelo said to pack my shit and beat it.

As a Yankees fan, I remember Yogi Berra's famous quote, "It's déjà vu all over again." Life for me is a circle, it seems. Back to his apartment and back to the diner where I worked and met my ex-girlfriend, Dawn.

Without the strength to walk anywhere else—I don't want to spend money on another cab either—to "Betty's Diner" I go.

Chapter Twenty-Three

Heads turn when I enter Betty's. Or I might be just too damn subconscious. It's hard not to think the customers are saying to themselves, *Another homeless guy in for a cup of coffee and a piece of pie.* As a short-order cook and occasional busboy for the owners, Betty and Joe, I used to stare, too.

Prices there are reasonable and the food's good, so this place is one stop for the homeless in Cedar's Point. I avoided the diner, until now, like the plague because of Dawn and too many memories, mostly bad ones.

Despite heavy foot traffic, the restaurant is clean. Betty and Joe insist on that from the staff. I've got no quarrels with them since they treated me right and didn't fire me until the cops took me away for a trip to the criminal justice system and prison.

Even with a weed and pill addiction, I usually showed up for work on time. When I didn't, there were lots of excuses. Another tell for an addict: we make pretty good con jobs. Nor did I flirt with Dawn too much as we both went about our business, cooking, cleaning, and waiting on tables and the counter.

Like a page from the fifties, Betty's has lots of chrome and windows. The sun's rays bounce off its smooth rounded corners from its key location only a few blocks from the harbor. The diner is busy when I select a booth even though it's before the peak dinner hour.

I look around and see neither Betty nor Joe. As a couple now in their late sixties, they've slowed down and trust their daughter to manage the place in their absence.

From the corral that also holds ketchup, sugar, salt and pepper, I grab a menu. Out of habit, I turn the dial to flip the selections on the old-style mini-jukebox that anchors each table. From Sinatra to Elvis to the Stones to the Eagles and much more, for only a quarter, diners can listen to the oldies and classics.

The swinging door to the kitchen pops open and there she is. I lift the menu to shield my face and peek over the top. Dawn is still as beautiful as ever. With hair darker than mine, her skin is perfect. Almost angelic white. Often joking that although we shared shades of black hair, Dawn would burn when we went to the ocean and I would tan.

She of Irish heritage and me with Italian genes. Her green eyes, button-like nose, and small mouth with full lips—that I loved to kiss—are well proportioned on her face. As a woman of five-nine with above average breasts and long legs, I miss those days of hanging with her at the beach or the bars. Dawn was all mine until *I* fucked up and she tossed me out.

As she comes to my booth, I lower the menu and to my surprise she smiles. Not sure what I expected. Water in the face. A kick to the balls. Both of which I deserve by the way. I return her smile and then tear up.

Her kindness unleashes a wall of emotion at the sight of the one good thing that happened after Mama evicted me. In a flash, I feel the longing for Dawn and the security of what used to be. Instead of what is now—the nights living scared in the woods, the attack, the cop chasing me away from the harbor because I'm out of place. All I want to do is hold her in my arms.

The air smells good from her subtle perfume that wafts about, I don't remember the brand. Conscious of how I appear and relieved that I'm clean from showering at Angelo's, out of nervous habit, I scratch my beard, something I did not have when my ex and I lived together.

Dawn smiles again and touches my left hand that's resting on the table. "Hi, Tony, it's good to see you," she says.

As I gaze into her eyes, I say, "I've missed you, Dawn. You look really amazing." Even in her black and white stodgy waitress uniform, she lights up a room. I struggle to fight back the passion roaring inside me.

"You, too. The beard and mustache give you a Viking vibe. How've you been?" she says, keeping the conversation purposely light.

"Getting by. Outta prison since spring. Drifted pretty much since then. Tough finding work with a record other than the car wash over on Route 15. The owner there is fair, and the tips aren't bad. Not enough to pay rent, though." I say.

Dawn hesitates for a moment and then sits down in the booth across from me. "I'm due for a short break. Lemme take your order, you eat, and then we can step outside and catch up for a few minutes. Not good to talk in here," she adds.

The restaurant is crowded now, and I know there's stuff she wants to ask, including if I'm using again. For Dawn, this is the sixty-four-thousand-dollar question.

I order a burger and a Diet Coke. For a flicker in time, I think about having a beer but that passes. Sobriety is a daily struggle to a point the doc in the hospital wouldn't prescribe opiates for my head pain—over-the-counter pills only—since at intake I'd shared that I am a recovering addict.

If prison did anything, it helped me get clean. I should attend more meetings, but I haven't been a regular and my sponsor and I have lost touch.

In less than five minutes, Dawn brings the order. This would have been something I cooked when I worked at Betty's. The food smells great and I dive in, enjoying every bit of this diner cuisine.

Chapter Twenty-Four

Dawn brings the check and I hand her the ten and tell her to keep the change. We step outside and walk across the street to a park with several benches and a statue of a Revolutionary War hero that hailed from this area.

For a few minutes, we sit in silence next to each other. Small talk in the restaurant is one thing. Anything serious requires us to open up to each another. The stillness is both awkward and yet we both feel a bond remains after living together for over a year.

I start the conversation because I owe her that. Dawn was the "victim" in the relationship because of my bad behaviors. "I'm really sorry for what I put you through. While life is hard, I've been sober for 251 days. I know throwing me out wasn't easy, but I deserved it. The lies, pills, stealing, cheating on you. All of it…Please forgive me." I wipe away the tears and choke back a sob.

To support my addiction, I took metal to scrap for cash. That and drug possession when the cops picked me up landed me in prison. "Careless" with the theft, through an investigation, the police nabbed me and others who had been taking aluminum and copper from wherever we could find it: abandoned buildings, people's yards, dumpsters, and commercial properties.

The more I used, the more I stole to reach new highs. And the more I caused Dawn to pull away.

The apology touches Dawn and she puts her arm around my shoulder. I lean my head into the nook of her neck and soft shoulder and the floodgates open: sorrow for the hurt I created, self-pity for my lot in life, hopelessness.

The flow of water is cleansing and the warmth of another person, someone I loved, provides healing and hope that better days are ahead.

Like this for a few minutes, she also runs her free hand through my hair. She always liked my thick mane and I'm content for the first time in months. Dawn's silence and actions are an acceptance of the ask for forgiveness and that comforts me.

After a while I speak. "How are ya? Seeing anyone? I hope you're happy," I add.

She says, "I'm in a good place, Tony, with a nice boyfriend. We're not living together or anything, but he treats me well. Steve works for the county as a deputy sheriff…" Her voice trails off, worried that she's gone too far.

I realize that people walking by the park see me resting against her. No sense screwing up her good thing by someone seeing us and reporting it to her boyfriend. I straighten up and wipe away the tears. Dawn hands me a tissue from her pocket and I blow my nose.

After receiving this news, I know I'm in no position

to lay any claim on her or our past life. "You deserve to be happy and deserve a good guy. Thanks for listening. Don't worry about me. I'll be fine," I say. Masculine instinct of "manning up" takes over.

"Take care of yourself, Tony. Glad we talked. Better get back before I'm missed." She reaches into her pocket again and I think to myself, *Please don't pull out money to give me. This has been humbling enough.*

Instead, Dawn writes her number on a piece of scrap paper and hands it to me. "If something comes up and you need a ride or have an emergency, call me, and Steve and I will try to help." Smart of her to add her boyfriend.

After thanking her, we hug. Dawn gets up and heads to Betty's. At the entrance to the restaurant, she turns and smiles and waves. I nod my head and smile back.

A good encounter, I bow my head and take a moment to thank God for healing, recognizing that my trek towards Him has taken an important step forward. Not only did I apologize to Dawn but in my heart to God as well for all the bad actions and sins of the past. Overcome with emotion, I ask Jesus to be my Savior, knowing I can't make it on this journey without Him. I'm filled immediately with a peace and calm I haven't experienced ever as the Lord's spirit works within me.

Exhausted from my time with Dawn and my talk with God, I walk back to Angelo's. If there's a sock on the knob, I'll sit on the front steps of the apartment building until given the "all clear" sign.

CHAPTER TWENTY-FIVE

From Tony's Journal
August 24, 2015
Day 103 of Homelessness

True to his word, Angelo boots me out after two days. The extra time to rest and sleep on a comfortable sofa helped my body heal. Before I leave, my cousin hands me a twenty-dollar gift card to the convenience store. Angelo makes a point of saying that while I claim to be clean, he's not taking any chances by handing over cash.

I understand his concerns. A suspicion not only of his but others because so many addicts slip back into the old life even when swearing they're not using. There seems to be a common misconception that alcoholism and drug addiction cause homeless. Not always. Often, the reverse is true. The despair drives a lot to substance abuse. At least from what I've encountered so far.

On the way home to the woods, I stop at the Methodist Church and Mrs. Seidel fills my food and toiletry requests. After I tell her about the attack and hospital stay, she asks another volunteer to take over so that we can step into the church sanctuary to pray. If it were anyone else, I'd be a little reticent about an open display of religion, but I trust this lady completely.

In the pew we sit, and Mrs. Seidel and I hold hands and then she prays. "Lord, I lift up Tony to you. Please heal his body and comfort him and provide strength to continue. Help him stay sober and to find sustenance and housing. In Jesus name. Amen."

With an extra squeeze of my hand, she tells me to take faith that God loves me. Misty-eyed, I thank this lady who has become such an important part of my life now.

CHAPTER TWENTY-SIX

Before leaving, I ask if there is anything I can do to help the pantry or church. Immediately she understands I'm looking for a small way to "pay" them back for their kindness even though that is never asked for.

She points to a broom and tells me I can sweep their fellowship hall and take out the garbage from the cans. Glad to have something to do, the work makes me feel like I'm part of the congregation. Part of something bigger than myself.

As I get ready to pack up, Mrs. Seidel comes over and asks whether I want to stay for the Bible study about to begin. She calls over their pastor, Lisa, a pretty woman in her forties, who gives me a warm smile and hug. I recoil a little since I have no experience with women as ministers.

The nuns I remember from my youth were stern and demanding. This preacher is neither. Pastor Lisa points to a table with hot coffee and pastries and tells me to help myself while handing me a Bible from a nearby desk.

After grabbing a donut and pouring a black coffee, I take a seat on the outside of the circle of parishioners that is forming. This is all new. Raised Catholic, I rarely opened a Bible and relied on the priests to lead us through Mass, reciting what they drilled into me to prepare for Confirmation and First Holy Communion.

The group is studying the Book of Matthew and what the pastor calls the "Sermon on the Mount." Rather than reading the words in the Bible, since I'm not sure where to find the text, I listen intently. Jesus's emphasis on blessing the poor appeals to me.

Afterwards, Pastor Lisa asks if I have a Bible. With my head down, I answer, "No." She says not to be ashamed and goes to her office, returning with a new Bible contained in a clean white box.

With another hug, Pastor Lisa also says Jesus loves me. I grab for my things to make the trek back home to the woods, with a warmth inside from hearing God's Word and receiving the love of these Christian folks.

Looking forward to arriving home to my campsite, I'm tired and need rest. The lean-to will need reassembly around the old concrete culvert first. As I approach the location in the thick forest, I see a large tent erected whose entrance leads to the nearby pipe.

This was one of my greatest fears that another homeless person would "poach" this spot and my face is flush from a building anger I might have to fight for what used to be mine. I back off to a safer place to wait and observe.

After about ten minutes, an older man exits the tent. Short and scruffy, his hair is all white. African American, he's probably in his sixties and walks with a limp and a demeanor that suggests this guy is even more beaten down than me. I watch him pull some items out of the pack leaning inside the culvert. And then he lights a pipe.

Time to either retreat or confront. With no energy to find a new campsite, I approach him in a friendly but firm manner. No match for me if things get testy, I hope he's not armed, however.

Chapter Twenty-Seven

With my right hand outstretched to shake his to prove I'm not holding a weapon, I say, "Yo, man. This is my spot. I got outta the hospital recently and need to grab some rest."

Standing next to him, his clothes are dirty, and his thick glasses don't seem to be working too well. Despite being short, he's not heavyset but rather thin and gaunt in the face and body.

"I was through here a few weeks ago and saw your camp. Since it was cleaned out, thought you'd moved on, young man. I mean no harm. Name is James." We shake.

"Tony's mine. Okay, you're still gonna have to find somewhere else to stay." Much older and obviously struggling, an inner voice is building deep within me to show him some pity, instead of attitude. I regret my words after they tumble out.

"Didn't look like you had a tent before. Happy to share mine, Tony. This is a good spot with the culvert and all. Some company would be nice. How long ya been homeless and lonely?" he asks, a smart way to divert my intention from tossing him out.

"Over 103 days. Not that I'm counting or anything," I chuckle. "I've gotten used to being on my own. We don't know each other, James. I've been attacked and treated pretty shitty, if you know what I mean."

"Homeless off and on for many years now, Tony. Had a tentmate years ago, and it was good to pool our things and take care of each other. You don't have a tent, right? Winter's comin', and I got a little inside heater, too. Please don't make me pack up. This place is close to everything but secluded and the old pipe gives some cover," he says.

Out of weariness, I paw at my face with my big hands. That same inside voice nudges me to accept. "Alright, we'll try it out. If it doesn't work, you gotta find somewhere else to camp." I say this but realize I can't push this guy along.

Physically, he looks weak and I can sense a bond forming between us. I also recognize I'm lonely. While Angelo and Belinda are a pain in the ass, it was good to be part of a family—even if for a brief period—rather than the "Lone Traveler" I've been for too long now.

James grins and for the first time I notice he's missing teeth. Not uncommon for the homeless since dental care is expensive. The diet can be crappy with lots of carbs and sweets that'll rot the teeth out after a while.

"Lemme show you the place," he says. Through the culvert we go to the inside of the tent—he's connected the two with a tarp overhead to help keep the entrance dry. I must admit it's a better set up than my old lean-to.

There's a pride evident in James as he conducts the tour. "I'll move my stuff to one side. Pick your half. The tent's patched up but dry and, in the winter, the little heater, with lots of layers on, helps although it's still damn cold. Old friend who was homeless found housing and gave it to me," he adds.

Rectangular, there is duct tape here and there. About eight by ten, I can stand in the middle but not so much at the edges. The right side has a better view of the entrance and pipe, so I choose it. James picks up his shit and tells me to make myself at home.

From the duffel bag I take the tarps and lay them down to provide extra cover for the sleeping bag and blankets. I pull from the knapsack a granola bar and my journal and pen. James is gazing at me. "Want some beef jerky, Tony?" he hands me a stick. "Whatcha writing?"

"Thanks. Yeah, I'm kinda hungry. Had a donut at the food pantry and that's it." I take a bite of the salted meat and it's tasty. "Where'd you get this? Not bad."

"At the convenience store. I seen you over there, I think."

"Every mornin' I go there until I was jumped. Watch your back in the parking lot, James. Tough gang of teenagers tryin' to mug homeless people." I'm already becoming protective of him.

"Will do." He stares at my book and I realize I haven't answered him.

"This is my journal." I hold it up. "Hope to be a writer some day and I'm chronicling my experiences," I add.

He laughs. "Am I gonna be in the story?"

I join him in laughing. "You are now. Want your real identity or a fake one?"

"Named after my father, Tony. I'm a junior. Proud of his name." As he points to the pipe, he says, "This here corn cob was his. The only thing I have left from him. Daddy's been gone for a long time." James shakes his head slightly and a sadness envelops him at the memory of his pop.

"How old are ya, man?" I say.

"You tell me," James counters.

While I don't want to offend the guy, I decide honesty must be the basis of this relationship from the beginning. "Your sixties, right?"

"Forty-nine." *Time and living on the streets has not been good to my new friend*, I observe to myself.

"Sorry. Never was like great with ages," I mumble, embarrassed I've given him so many more years.

"It's okay. I try not to look in a mirror in the restroom 'cause I look old."

James turns and lays down on the cot. A Bible is by his pillow. He pulls out a magnifying glass and puts it over the words. "Look at that much?" I say.

"Yep. This little book and I been through a lot together." With a reverence, he pats the worn leather binding with "Holy Bible" stamped in gold over the top.

"Any time you wanna borrow it, Tony, it's here on my cot."

"I got one, too," I say with pride. I pull the new book

Dave Transue

from the knapsack and point to it. "The Methodist Church gave me it."

"Haven't been over there in a while. Nice people."

Seeing James lay down, I write for only a while. And then stretch out on my "bed" and look up to the ceiling with a flap open that allows a view of the sky as it's filtered through the trees. The streams of light piercing the evergreen canopy are almost heavenly in nature, perfect for the peace I've found from having a new friend.

Something is just right about this new arrangement and even though it's still daylight out, I close my eyes and change my prayer, adding James—thanking God for giving me some company in this lonely journey.

As if reading my mind, he says, "Nite, Tony. Sleep well. Thanks for teaming up."

"You, too, James. This is a nice set up you got." An approaching late afternoon thunderstorm provides a natural lullaby. The low rumblings from the western sky are somehow soothing. Dry and cozy, I've made a new bud.

I drift off to a deep slumber for the first time while living in the woods. The loneliness and feeling that I'm going to be attacked while I sleep is lessened.

CHAPTER TWENTY-EIGHT

From Tony's Journal
September 25, 2015
Day 135 of Homelessness

James and I settle into an easy routine. Clean, considerate, kind, funny, wise, he's become my best pal. In many ways, my only close friend. Doing everything together, we've got each other's back.

"Wingmen" to one another in every sense. As a pair, we are safer, and the ridicule and stares aimed at the homeless are easier to shake off. The story of how each of us became homeless slowly comes out. Not all at once but in pieces.

Over fifteen years ago, James had a wife and two children and a decent job as a heavy equipment operator. When he caught his wife having an affair, his bad temper flared, and he struck her and was arrested, doing time for this battery and later for failure to pay child support.

I can't help wondering how this mild-mannered man would ever strike his wife. Or anyone for that matter. This quiet, decent, religious man has clearly undergone a complete transformation from those dark days.

After losing his family and the prison stint, he says things really went south. The bottle and he had a great love affair until his employer at that time had had enough, firing James for showing up late to work and sleeping on the job because he was hungover all the time. The little savings he had dried up, and he couldn't afford rent any longer.

Like me, he's estranged from his family. No contact now for many years, there's a deep sorrow around his brown eyes when he talks about his wife and kids and wonders aloud how they're doing; what kind of life have they had without him?

James has become the father I never had. If he were alive, my dad would be a decade or so older than my friend. I didn't know Papa all that well and James helps me understand—without making excuses for Stanley Jankowski—that life can be very hard for a sole provider working in monotonous jobs as Papa and James did.

Mama didn't work while my father was alive, and James explains that this put lots of pressure on Papa to meet the bills and needs of two children he and Mama had to raise. As I described our dreary row home, James also gives insights that Papa probably felt like a failure but couldn't express it other than through drinking and eating to excess and lots of yelling.

CHAPTER TWENTY-NINE

September has brought an "Indian Summer." After making it through the heat and stickiness of June, July, and August, this last blast of summer is not welcome. As I write in my journal, James is reading God's Word. We talk a lot about the Bible and my connection to the Lord grows through James and his wisdom.

So comfortable with one another, because there's little air flowing, and the humidity is stifling, we've stripped down to our underwear. We drink a lot of water and made the convenience store run at dawn, knowing the temperature would rise quickly to make any movement more strenuous with each passing hour.

This kind of fluid intake causes frequent trips to the adjoining woods to pee and James and I make sure we do not do so too close to the campsite, trying to keep the area clean and smelling of pine only!

On Medicaid, James also gets about forty dollars a month from food stamps. Not enough to feed him, also like me, he's on the circuit of pantries and soup kitchens run by the area's churches. We probably ran into each other at one time or another but paid no attention since there's a stream of homeless that interact without always knowing names or even paying mind to faces either.

James says he's tried for housing. But the system and the flood of paper that comes with seeking government assistance caused him to give up. With his bad eyes, he also filed for disability but didn't meet the legal definition of blindness.

Sometimes he'll find odd jobs, pushing carts at the supermarket or cleaning offices and homes. His limp makes it difficult to work, however, so his income is even more limited than mine—at least I have the car wash tips as a source of money.

James also shows me the wide scar on his right leg—the cause of the limp—from a serious wound suffered on the job site where he almost lost his leg. Consulting a lawyer, he thought there was a good case for worker's compensation and damages. The company lawyered up and the history of his drinking became the key issue and he got nothing.

A friend of his holds James's mail at his address and James says he's sure I could have mail sent there, too. I intend to take advantage of this since a place to receive mail is a problem when you're homeless.

The flip phone rings, interrupting my writing. A rarity. It's Angelo who never, ever calls. This can't be good. The journal will have to wait.

Chapter Thirty

"Yo, Angelo."

"Cuz, can't talk long since I'm on break at the shop. Your mom called my mom. Cassandra's in bad shape, dude. Hit by a car real bad and she's in a coma. You'd better get home to see her."

For a long moment, I'm too stunned to respond. "Did ya hear me, Tony? You gotta get back north. NOW," he says.

"Yeah, I heard ya already, Angelo. Give me a second, would ya? This is a lot to take in, bro."

"I gotta go, man," he says.

"Wait, can I get a lift after you're finished work? A bus will take too long, and I don't have the money to—"

"Can't do that, dude. Belinda and I are hangin' out tonight. I'll call my mom that you're makin' plans. Bye." Like that, he's gone again as quickly as he came back into my life. I guess I should be grateful there's at least some connection with my family. Even as thin as it is through my cousin.

I'd gone outside to answer the call and went back

into the tent and sat down on the cot I'd purchased from Walmart with some of the money saved up for my own tent. In just my underwear, I cry. The tears fall hard onto my bare chest.

Cassie is six years younger than me. That would make her seventeen now and I curse myself for not remembering her birthday. Other than knowing she's in a coma, I'm in the dark and frustrated as hell I can't get home.

James comes over and puts his hand on my shoulder. "What's wrong, Tony? What happened on that call?"

"My sister's in a coma. From a car hitting her. Doesn't sound good, James. How am I supposed to get to the hospital? Angelo's too damn busy with that bitch of a girlfriend of his."

"I'll pray for her and your mom. In fact, let's pray now and we'll figure things out after we go to the Lord. Now is not the time for anger but for quiet…so we can hear Him."

Two grown men in nothing but skivvies, black and white, young and old, kneel on the tent floor and join hands. "Heavenly Father," Tony begins. "We don't understand why these things happen. This tragedy is beyond our knowledge. Cassie needs your healing, Lord, if that is your will. Please give comfort and strength, Jesus, for Cassie and Tony's mama, and help Tony find a way home. In Jesus name we pray. Amen."

Too weak from overwhelming emotions, I can't say, "Amen," but allow the streaming tears to seal the prayer as my agreement with James's words. Last week, I remember him reading scripture from Jesus that when two or more join in prayer, it will be done by the Father in Heaven.

My roommate reads my thoughts. "Now, we're gonna believe, Tony. Cassandra is in His loving arms and care."

CHAPTER THIRTY-ONE

Young in my faith travel and only just understanding what Christianity is all about, I thank James. But I can't shake the image in my mind of my baby sister getting hit and laying in a hospital bed in a coma, hooked up to all sorts of machines, with tubes coming out of her. With me over seventy miles away and without a car.

Anger and guilt follow the initial shock and anguish and I go outside the tent to a nearby pine tree and slam my fist into it, shouting, "This is fuckin' bullshit."

The blood flowing from my knuckles is easier to endure than these other emotions. Deep within my being, I want to resort back to the "Old Tony," the one who fought, drank, did drugs, and let his fists do his talking. I want to become again the "animal" Mama threw out over two-and-a-half years ago. These were all mechanisms I realize now were emotional defenses against getting close to anyone, including my mother and sister.

James comes outside and gently guides me back into our tent. He grabs for my jeans and a shirt and tells me to get dressed. Almost robotic at this point, I do as he says.

He also says to light up a cigarette and to sit on my cot. The old corncob pipe comes out and James packs it full of tobacco. I pull a smoke from the pack and James flicks the lighter for me and for his pipe. After a deep drag, I run my hand through my hair, in need of a good washing as the grease slides through my fingers.

Despite this being day 285 of sobriety, I long for weed and a beer and say that to James. Shaking his head, he says, "That won't do no good for the situation. Stay strong and sober."

Across from me on his bunk, James provides additional direction, knowing I'm not thinking clearly. "Have that cigarette and take a drink of water," he says. Throwing me a towel, he tells me to wrap my hand—I'd forgotten about my banged-up fist.

"Stop the bleedin' and then we'll clean that up." I notice some swelling and wish we had ice to doctor with but that's a luxury we can't afford.

James continues. "Okay, we've gotta get ya home. Think about the friends you have in this area. Someone, besides Angelo, who could give a lift on short notice."

In the fog of tobacco smoke, I close my eyes, continue inhaling on the cigarette, and ponder the possibilities. *Mrs. Seidel is too old to make the trip up the Garden State Parkway and New Jersey Turnpike where one needs nerves of steel to drive. While she'd come to my rescue with no hesitation, I couldn't put her through that experience,* I decide.

And then it comes to me. Dawn and her boyfriend. She'd given me the number and said to call in an emergency.

"What 'bout my ex-girlfriend?" I say to James. My way of making sure this isn't a terrible idea.

"From what you've told me, you two had a nice talk, and you apologized for all the bad behavior. Make the call, Tony."

For the first time, I think about James and leaving him. "How 'bout you?" I can feel my face notched up in wrinkled concern as I ask this.

"Don't worry. I've been on my own for a long time. Call Dawn and get home," he says.

Soon the cigarette is just a stub and I put it out and pull out my wallet. There's the piece of paper with Dawn's handwriting. I hesitate. Do I have the right to ask her for anything?

James sees the indecision. "Call her. She wouldn't have given you that if she didn't mean it."

For some crazy reason, I borrow James's small mirror and comb my hair. I take off the towel and use a couple of baby wipes to clean off my fist. James wraps a bandage around it from his first aid kit.

Off my shirt goes and I use a few towelettes to rub off the dirt and stench that's thick on my torso. A swab of deodorant under each arm and I feel readier to make the call—not that Dawn will see me over my simple flip phone but I'm conscious of my appearance around her. No longer the "stud" anymore that she used to live with, I do my best to look presentable.

"Better, James?"

"Yeah, you're good, Tony. Ya got this."

CHAPTER THIRTY-TWO

Between my nervousness over making this call to Dawn and how worried I am about Cassandra, my hands are shaking. Once again, James takes charge. After finding his trusty magnifying glass, he dials the number from the paper I've handed him.

Giving the flip phone back to me, he says, "It's ringing."

"Hello," Dawn answers.

"Uh, it's Tony. Hey."

"Everything okay, Tony? Are you hurt again?"

Together long enough she knows I'm in trouble, I say, "It's Cassie, Dawn. Angelo called. A car hit her and she's in a coma. I need to get home but have no ride…" My deep voice falls off. Tearing up again, James hands me a tissue.

"Steve and I'll drive you back north, Tony. I'm so sorry. He's off today and I'll be finished work soon. Where can we get you?"

"The convenience store on Wake Street. Do you know it? We live only about ten minutes from there."

"Who's we? Never mind. We can catch up later. Yeah,

I'm sure Steve knows where it is." I remember he's in law enforcement so that makes sense.

"Tell me when to meet you there," I say.

"How 'bout an hour? We'll be in a black Ford SUV."

"Can't thank you enough, Dawn. There's no way I could do this without your help."

"No worries. See you soon, Tony."

I turn to James. "She said, 'yes.'"

He nods. "God is good."

"I'm wiped, man. Need to lie down for a few minutes. Can you wake me in a half hour?"

"Sure, get some rest."

The time goes by fast, and James nudges my cot. "Time to get up and get ready, bud."

With a rub to my face, I swing my legs over my bed to put on my shoes. But first, I pull my life savings, about 140 dollars, out of my left shoe. Twenty dollars is all I figure I need.

I give the rest to James, who I trust with my treasure. "Take this for safe-keeping, please. Don't wanna travel to the city with too much cash on me."

"Come here," James says. His arms are wide open, and we embrace. Since I tower over him, I rest my head down sideways on his shoulder. I well up and sob. *Thank you, God, for this man,* I say to myself.

Some clothes, toiletries, and snacks packed in my knapsack, I'm ready. James tells me, "Now go, Tony. You don't wanna be late. I'll be here waitin' for you."

Between Cassandra's situation and leaving my friend

behind, I've got this large pit in my stomach as I walk out of the tent. *Steady me, Lord, for what lies ahead,* I pray.

The ten-minute trip seems like ten hours. Lost in a haze as I make my way to the store, the past races through my thoughts. Mama, Cassandra, Dawn, Angelo, Mrs. Schnitzer, Mrs. Seidel. And now James. All the people who've been a part of my short life. And all the bad stuff I've done also comes to the fore.

At the convenience store, I lean against the side wall and light a cigarette. I remind myself to write about the trip back home. A writer writes from his or her experiences, my English teacher always told us. Aloud I say, "I hope my baby sister's okay and Mama isn't still pissed."

CHAPTER THIRTY-THREE

From Tony's Journal
September 26, 2015
Day 136 of Homelessness

As I write this, I'm hungover. Forgive me for any errors. With a pounding head, I'm torqued at myself for drinking. Yes, I must start all over again with sobriety. Day one of another daily challenge to remain sober. If James were here, I'd have stayed clean but there was no one to pull me back from the abyss.

Laying on the cot in the back room of Sal's Bar, I need to move on to find a different place to sleep. More on that later.

Dawn and Steve picked me up at the convenience store as promised. Steve could be a prototypical cop: big, muscular, high and tight haircut, intense eyes that constantly scan for danger. I like him. Despite the fierce persona, we hit it off. Since he's a deputy sheriff, he's got familiarity with the homeless in the area and a sensitivity that's lacking in some cops.

The ride went smoothly, and they dropped me off at the hospital that serves my native city. Dawn hugged me, and

Steve gave me a firm handshake, planting a twenty in my hand as he did so.

They explained they're going away on vacation and wouldn't be able to drive me back to Cedar's Point. "I'll be fine and figure something out," I said to assure them. Besides, at that point, I had no idea how long my stay would be.

After entering the hospital, I asked for directions and the volunteer pointed me to intensive care on the seventh floor. The trip in the elevator was maddeningly slow as doctors, nurses, orderlies, and visitors entered and exited on each floor. Finally, I reached the destination.

At the nurse's station, I told them I'm Cassandra Jankowski's brother. After I produced ID, the head nurse pointed to the family waiting area. A very unpleasant woman, and not like those who took care of me during my hospitalization, she told me to wait until my mother came out. And here's how that encounter and the aftermath went. Blow by blow by blow.

CHAPTER THIRTY-FOUR

I brace myself for the first meeting with Mama in over two years. Even though I'm a changed man, she doesn't know that. Nor does she understand what the struggles of addiction, prison, and homelessness have done to my soul. Forced to grow up fast, I'm far wiser now than my twenty-three years.

After about twenty minutes of waiting, Mama comes out of the unit. With her is Mrs. Ortenzio. I involuntarily shiver at the sight of this tag-team of old Italian woman as if a cold current of mountain water courses through my veins, anticipating the verbal beating to come.

Mama is in the same black dress she wore to bury Papa and throw me out. Mrs. Ortenzio is also in black— she's replaced the old flowery dress and her trademark scarf with a plain frock and black Turban hat graced with a large red rose.

At the sight of that goofy hat, I couldn't help but imagine Mrs. Ortenzio as one of those psychics that advertises on late night television. A crystal ball in front of her with tarot cards to back up her "findings." If I were the subject for the reading of the tea leaves, she would predict my demise, because of the hatred she holds against me deep within her core. Even if her occult readings said otherwise.

I hug Mama, and she and Mrs. Ortenzio scowl. Mama does not reciprocate by putting her arms around me. Stiff as a board, she merely says, "Anthony," as her form of greeting. *So much for a fresh start* goes through my mind.

Mrs. Ortenzio curses something in Italian, not "*Feccia*," or scum, however, her usual term of endearment for my existence.

This visit is tough enough but these two aren't going to make it any easier. "How's Cassie and when can I see her?" I say to move the conversation along.

Mama answers with tears in her eyes, "In a coma. It doesn't look good."

Tears start in my eyes, and that startles Maria Jankowski. She'd never seen me cry or show any emotion except anger, especially in the teen years leading up to my eviction. "Can we sit for a few minutes to talk before I visit Cassie?" I say.

With great reluctance she agrees although Mrs. Ortenzio tries to join in, and I said, "Please, Mama, alone?"

Mama's friend glares in a menacing fashion. As if to signal—Hurt her, and I hurt you—before she walks away.

CHAPTER THIRTY-FIVE

Mama and I sit, and I hold her hand in mine. While her head shakes in disgust, she says, "You've been an awful brother. My baby girl's all banged up. So beautiful. So smart. So good. Cassandra's everything you aren't. Where did I go wrong with you, Anthony?"

While this is devastating, just like with Dawn, I deserve every bit of it. And then some. Insensitive and selfish when I lived with her, I owe her an explanation. "Mama, I've changed. It's been a tough time but I'm not the same kid you kicked out. Between prison and—"

Mama shrieks. "I knew you'd end up there," she says.

"Lemme finish, please. I did bad stuff and paid a price. I've been homeless, too, and I'm ready to come home to help with the house, the bills, and my sister. Cassie's gonna recover, right?" I say.

"No, Anthony. There's been too much bleeding. The doctors don't think she'll last long now. I only called through your cousin, so you could try to make your peace. God knows you have much to answer for to your sister and your mama. Father Mario will be here soon for the last rites."

With a harder squeeze to her hand, we both sob. Mama—because she's losing her daughter. Me—because I'll never see my baby sister conscious again.

"When I go in, Mama, I'll pray with Cassie, too. I've been reading the Word of God and goin' to a Bible study at the Methodist Church. James, my tentmate, also has been teachin' me."

Maybe this will be a breakthrough, I think.

Mama straightens up in the chair and says with a new glimmer in her eyes, "To Mass? You've rejoined the faith?"

"Not exactly but I'm tryin' to understand the Lord." Might as well have said I'm a practicing believer in Zoroastrianism because that is what it seems Maria Jankowski heard. Methodists are as foreign to her as Judaism would be.

"What does that mean, son? All that religious training when you were younger..." The tears stop like they are on a switch. And she is mad again. With a dismissive wave of her hand, she says, "Go see your sister before she slips away."

Mrs. Ortenzio returns and wags a finger at me. I couldn't help myself but mutter, "Eavesdropping little bitch." Add one more charge to the rap sheet held by the neighborhood florist lady who always brings out the worst in me.

The nasty nurse takes me back to Cassie's room. Between the beeping noises and ventilator tube, I'm freaked out. George, my roommate in the hospital, was bad but nothing like this.

Cassie is unresponsive. With a damaged and bloated face, I don't recognize her. Before the accident, she was beautiful with long black hair and olive skin, only just beginning her journey as she blossomed into a spectacular young woman when I left home.

I tried to remember her as the little kid who only wanted to hang out with her brother. The girl who played hopscotch on the sidewalk in front of our home. The happy child who blew bubbles in the alley and laughed and laughed in delight. The considerate girl who helped Mama with housework while I sat around and expected to be waited on.

By her bedside, I take her hand into mine, leaning my face into our clasp. Tears wash over the union of our hands. "So sorry, sis. Should've been there for ya."

Ten minutes pass. Father Mario enters. We shake hands and he's as stern as I remember him from my altar boy days.

"One more minute, Father?" I say, understanding he needs to do his thing.

He says, "Time is short, Anthony."

Back to holding her hand, I pray, "Lord, I'm like not really good at this. Please take the pain away from Cassie. Fill her with your love. In Jesus name. Amen."

I cross myself, kiss Cassie's forehead, and leave. I don't want to witness Father Mario's administration of the last rites. That finality is too much to endure and I pass

Mama and Mrs. Ortenzio as they enter the room, both gripping their rosaries.

For another thirty minutes, I sit in the waiting room, scrawling in the journal, smudged even more from my tears. The trio of Father Mario, Mama, and Mrs. Ortenzio finally comes out. The priest says, "She's gone to be with God."

I try to hug Mama and Mrs. Ortenzio intervenes. "*No. Abbastanza. Devi andartene ora.*" Her turban is tilted from her head shaking so hard as she makes this pronouncement. The red rose, apparently only pinned on, is now hanging down over her left eye. If my sister hadn't just died, I'd have laughed in her face.

Only understanding basic Italian, all I recognize from her torrent of words is "No."

Father Mario translates. "Maria wants you to leave now, Tony. She's had enough."

Mama's back is to me as Mrs. Ortenzio comforts her. My hot Latin temper wants to erupt. To blast them all but what good would that have done? I grab my knapsack instead and head to the elevator.

Chapter Thirty-Six

From the lobby, I stumble out into the dark, drifting end-lessly on the streets of the old neighborhood. *Where will I sleep tonight*? I wonder. I don't care there is no answer. Hatred. Remorse. Bitterness. Sorrow. All overwhelm me.

I pass Sal's Bar and recognize it as Papa's old hangout. Even though I never drank there back in the day, I enter. Filled with older Italian gentlemen, I wonder how Stanley Jankowski made this his place as a Polish guy?

At the end of the nicked up dark walnut counter—I notice many names etched into the wood as patrons leave their mark they were there—the bartender comes over and introduces himself as the owner, Sal.

"Tony Jankowski's my name."

Sal breaks out in a big smile. "Are you Stanley's boy?"

"Yes, sir. Passing through town and decided to check out where my father spent most of his time."

"Glad you did, Tony. How long has your pop been gone?" he says.

"Over fourteen years," I say.

"Never met your mother but Stanley talked a lot about

her. Says he was a lucky man to have married a pretty Italian girl."

"Papa said that?!" I exclaim in surprise. It's hard for me to see Mama in that way. To me, she's an old scold and my father did nothing but yell and drink.

Sal nods his head vigorously in reaction to my wonderment. "Yep. Like other men that spend time here, he bitched about her and you kids. But Stanley loved your mother. Trust me."

"What'd he say 'bout me?"

Like a little kid again, I yearn for some approval or affirmation from what seems like only a ghost. A mere shadow whose photo sat on our dining room sideboard as a reminder there was a man in the house at one time.

"Said he was proud of the young man you were becomin', Tony. He was glad your mother insisted on religious education even though he didn't go to Mass much." As he mentions this, I remember arguments between Mama and Papa as she implored him to join us in going to church. Papa never did.

Sal is looking into the distance as he says this, almost as if he's picturing Stanley Jankowski back from the dead. The tap flows, my old man is shooting the shit with the guys again, and for a short time the cares of the world melt away at Sal's Bar. I can picture Papa dressed in his plant uniform—grungy from that day's work—his big belly straining against the curvature of the bar counter I now sit at.

I wipe away a tear, hoping Sal doesn't see it. *Enough*

sniveling already, Tony. Man up. You're where your father used to drink. Where he shot darts and told dirty jokes. He wouldn't be proud of how sensitive I've become, I conclude.

Stanley Jankowski was angry and sullen in our household but never, ever, was he a wimp.

CHAPTER THIRTY-SEVEN

Sal returns to the present and says, "What'll it be, Tony? First one's on the house. In honor of Stanley." He takes out a clean glass from under the bar.

In that moment, I don't give a shit about remaining sober. Pissed, hurt, and missing my little sister, it's time to drown these emotions in something that'll take the edge off.

"What kinda beer did Papa drink?" I say.

"Rolling Rock," Sal says. "Depending on how the day went at the plant, he'd have a shot to start, followed by the chaser."

"One of those then. With a shot of Fireball, please." I'm sure Papa had bourbon or Jack, but I am a millennial after all.

For the first time in a long time, I feel alive again. Eager to get drunk, *Maybe I can score weed, too,* runs through my mind.

Sal pours the shot and beer. I down both. Proud to slap the empty shot glass down against the bar…as a "real" man does.

The taste of that whisky and beer slides down my throat like honey. An elixir of the gods to bring Anthony Jankowski back to who he used to be. The thug who didn't give a shit about anything or anybody. And away from the sensitive, sniveling, considerate man I'd turned into because of life on the streets. Drifting and depending on the mercy of others. *What kinda fuckin' man have ya turned into, Tony?*

I check my wallet. Two twenties in there, including the money Steve gave me. On the counter, I smack the cash down hard. I'm a big man again—even if it's only temporary...till the coin runs dry.

In a few minutes the buzz builds—from my head all the way down to my toes. I tingle with nervous excitement at the sensation I haven't felt since entering prison. "Keep 'em comin', Sal," I say.

He sees how intense I am and says, "Something happen, Tony?"

"Yeah, my baby sister just crapped out," I tell him, almost mechanically.

With a nod of understanding, he tells me he's sorry for my loss. His look conveys a hardscrabble discernment that only an old bartender possesses. Good listeners, they've seen and heard it all. Death, divorce, cheating, foreclosure, layoffs. Sal has been a witness to it.

To distract me back to thinking about my old man, he says, "By the way, you're sittin' right where he used to. I think his name's carved there. Go ahead, put your name by his."

Sal hands me a knife from behind the counter. After finding Papa's name, and although my hand's a little unsteady from the alcohol, I carve in "Anthony Bennett Jankowski" in an open spot near his.

I lean down and kiss his carving, sealed with cinnamon whisky and beer. From son to father. From one addict to another. The generations continue getting stoned at Sal's Bar, a happy place away from the bullshit of life.

The booze continues to flow freely until my money runs out and I'm leaning over the bar. Barely conscious, I mumble something about Cassie and Mama and losing them again. Only it's permanent this time.

Then I think of James and I'm ashamed. If he could see me now, what would he say? I sob. All I utter is, "I'm sorry." Over and over again. Sorry for being a shithead in the past and sorry I'm so weak that I drank myself to oblivion.

Sal comes over and says, "C'mon, Tony. Sleep this off. You've got nowhere to stay, tonight, right?"

As he moves around the countertop, he pulls me off the stool and asks one of the other patrons to help him take me to the back room. Deadweight, they guide all 180 pounds of me to the rear of the building.

"You can't go home to your mother like this, Tony. I owe it to your father to let you sleep here," he says.

"I'm homeless, Sal. Have no home here and none at the Jersey Shore where I live in a fuckin' tent. Can you believe that shit? That bitch wants nothing to do with me" I blubber.

"Don't talk about your mama like that," Sal barks. "Your father would strike you hard if he heard that. Now pull yourself together, Tony. Bad things happen in life and you're a man...Stanley's son no less." The sympathy is over and I'm getting a pep talk from an old Italian bartender.

At the restroom they stop and take me into the urinal. Too drunk to care I'm about to piss in front of two old men, I yank my zipper down and take care of business.

Sal and his customer resume taking me to the back room. Papa's friend puts on a light and points to a cot. "Sleep there till morning, and I'll have coffee for you." I crash on the bunk and drift off to sleep immediately until morning comes.

And then it seems like "Red the Attacker" has struck with the baseball bat again.

Chapter Thirty-Eight

From Tony's Journal
September 28, 2015
Day 138 of Homelessness

I've hit rock bottom. Sal brewed coffee as promised and then said he was sorry he had to put me out. "Can't have tenants staying here long-term, Tony. The city might hassle my operation," he says.

After thanking him, I ask where the homeless shelter is, which is where I am writing from to catch up on my experiences. I needed to find a place to stay until I can secure a ride home. Sal gives me directions and a "to go" cup so I could be on my way.

The route to the shelter passes my old home where I stand out front for a while. "The House of Stanley and Maria Jankowski," I say out loud bitterly. With a page taken from Mrs. Ortenzio, I spit on the sidewalk. I will never return here. Ever. For Mama to reject me again is just too much to take.

The old high school alma mater seems smaller now and not much has changed as I pass it. Graffiti all over and lots of kids hanging out in the yard that's surrounded with a rusty chain-link fence. I think of Mrs. Schnitzer and vow to make her proud by writing this book. Finally, I reach the shelter.

At least three stories high, it takes up half a city block. All brick, there are windows with bars and large exhaust fans emitting smoke on the roof. Like the school, graffiti marks the building. Someone tried to paint a mural on one side as "urban art" but the street "artists" have sprayed over that, too.

A bunch of guys are hanging out at the entrance, smoking, and shooting the shit. With a nod of acknowledgement, I pass them. Nobody returns the courtesy.

I open the door and go to the front desk to check in. James had warned me that the big city shelters are crime and bug-infested. Early in his homelessness, he had stayed at one. Never again, he said. Now I understand why.

In fairness, after my experience, I've learned these shelters are underfunded, understaffed, and overwhelmed with the demand because so few exist for those living on the streets.

Chapter Thirty-Nine

Checked in by a volunteer who lacks any warmth or personality, he says, "Been here before?" I answer no.

He hands me a sheet of rules in large and bold print. No drugs or alcohol. No fighting. No sex. No profanity. No theft. "Violate these, we boot you. Understood?" he says.

"Yes, sir," I answer. He shoves across the desk another paper to sign, acknowledging the restrictions. I sign "Anthony Bennett Jankowski" on the dotted line. Many my age are signing apartment leases. Or better yet, mortgages for their first home. Instead, I'm signing for the opportunity to walk through the Gates of Hell.

To the bunk room we go. Over seventy-five cots spaced tightly together in the large gymnasium, I suspect there are more on the other floors.

"Bathrooms are over there," he says, pointing to the far right. "Find an open cot and make it yours." He leaves me on my own after that brief tour.

First, I head to the bathroom. Greeted by eight urinals and eight stalls, there are no doors on the stalls. *So much for privacy when you crap,* I note. *One more way to "dehumanize" the homeless.* Disinfectant and foul human smells assault my senses.

The mirrors have been removed as if those in charge have given up keeping them intact. In their place is a thin silver tin sheet over each sink. I stare at my image. As distorted as this place is, I feel like I'm in a "funhouse" with no exit.

Shaving would be hard here to do and I'm glad hair covers my face. Several of the sinks have men's stubble and mucus all over them. I want to vomit at the sight. In another room are the open showers with hooks outside the door to hang your towel.

Back out to the main room, I find an empty cot with a pillow and blanket. There's about three feet between my bunk and the guy's cot next to it.

My "bunkmate" seems to be in a daze as he looks up from his bed at the old industrial ceiling with its large fluorescent lights, blazing down like interrogation lamps in a police station.

Awake, his eyes are gray and lifeless. Dressed in military camouflage pants and a green wool shirt, dog tags hang around his neck and lay on his chest. With long matted hair, his is greasier than mine.

Not knowing how long I'll be here, I put my hand out, "Name's Tony. Nice to meet you."

Slowly, he looks over. "Steven," he says. His hand doesn't make a move towards mine as if it's too much effort for him to shake hands.

"Thanks for your service," I say, figuring I owe him at least that courtesy.

"You're welcome," Steven says as he turns over on his side, away from me to make it clear conversation is not appreciated.

The journal comes out of my knapsack and I stretch out on my cot to write. Anger builds within me as I think about how a country as great as this one can treat its vets like this. That this man, a hero, lives without hope in a homeless shelter is shameful.

Not knowing his circumstances, I'm quite sure the government shouldn't let thousands of men and women like him rot and not give a damn that this condition exists. James had said he's encountered many homeless veterans in his travels so I'm confident this veteran, sadly, is not alone in his suffering.

CHAPTER FORTY

Exhausted, I've had little sleep in this shelter. Too wired because I'm afraid to sleep, like a caged animal I pace around my cot and then to the outside to smoke and then back in again.

The sounds of exhaustion, despair, frustration, and anger are all around me. Nightmares in which people are yelling in their sleep, loud snores, profanity, and several fights that break out, are the noises of the stressful life that is homelessness in a big city shelter.

Steven has a cold and his coughing has spread the virus. So now I'm sick. If I remain in this place, I have the feeling I might catch something worse.

Other than using the toilet, I don't dare shower. I won't leave my knapsack behind on the cot nor do I want to be naked and vulnerable in the shower if a fight should break out in the bathroom. I can't help but think, too, what if a fire should start and I'm under the nozzle without clothes on? Then what?

On edge, I decide I must walk out of this hellhole and take my chances on the streets until I figure out a way to get home to James and the tent. A relative haven of security and peace I appreciate now more than ever.

With zero money and little food remaining in my pack, I bolt. *Holing up in one of the abandoned warehouses than staying at the "shelter" has gotta be better,* I conclude. I think about who's left that I know in the city besides family since that door is closed.

Then it comes to me. Mrs. Schnitzer has an adult daughter who I met several times after class when she was visiting her mother and once when we had a party to celebrate the end of the school year. Mrs. Schnitzer and her daughter made cupcakes with many of the literary great's names plastered over them to reinforce those authors she pointed to as inspirations for us to emulate.

I walk to my teacher's home, hoping her daughter has kept the house in the family. Even if she lives there, I'm not sure what her reaction will be to my showing up. She may not remember me.

Mrs. Schnitzer lived in a better neighborhood than ours but still modest especially compared to the oceanfront mansions of the Jersey Shore. A brick duplex, I walk up the steps and admire the neat porch with a wooden swing suspended from the ceiling and several wicker chairs framed by what look like large fern plants. With a welcoming entranceway, clearly the owner has pride in this home.

Chapter Forty-One

With a ring of the doorbell, I wait anxiously. The door cracks open and it's Mrs. Schnitzer's daughter who says, "Yes, can I help you?"

"Hi. I don't know if you remember me, but your mother was my creative writing teacher. I'm Tony Jankowski."

She breaks out into a big smile and opens the door and says, "Of course, I do, Tony. Come in and sit down."

I follow her into the nicely furnished living room. Several upholstered chairs face a brick fireplace with a painted white mantel that has framed family photos displayed, including of Mrs. Schnitzer. An upright piano sits in the corner and I remember my teacher saying she used to play piano and the organ at her church.

Next to it is a floor-to-ceiling bookcase loaded with books from the great authors: Hemmingway, Dickens, Melville, Salinger, Twain, Poe, Steinbeck, Fitzgerald. And so on. A literary treasure trove I could spend hours and hours reading—beyond those examples Mrs. Schnitzer used to inspire us.

"What brings you here, Tony? You know my mother passed away, right? She was always so fond of you and proud of how you took to writing."

The emotions well up within me at the mention of Mrs. Schnitzer and her pride in me. "I'm so sorry I forgot your name. But I'm in trouble and need help."

"Sharon. Lemme get you a cup of coffee and then we can talk." I welcome a break in the conversation to gather my wits.

After about five minutes, Sharon returns with a small tray of coffee, cream and sugar, and a pile of cookies I eye greedily since I've eaten very little since leaving the tent—the food at the shelter was not that appetizing so I passed on going through the serving line. I thank her for the hospitality.

"Okay, Tony, what's goin' on?"

Sharon is so open and earnest that my story pours out, in between munching on the food and drinking the coffee. She listens intently and asks several questions for clarification since I'm not thinking so clearly because of a lack of sleep and the turmoil of the last few days.

"I'm so sorry about your sister, Tony. Too young to die," she says as she shakes her head. "I'll pray for your mother and family. So, ya need a ride home, is that it?"

"Yeah, I have to get back to what I know and where I'm safer. There's nothing here for me any longer. I have no money left either."

"Finish your coffee, Tony, and take those cookies, please. I know you're hungry. We're going to the bus station." After a few more gulps of coffee, I stuff the treats in my knapsack. For the first time in days, I have hope.

Chapter Forty-Two

Sharon grabs her purse and keys and I follow her out to the porch. She locks the door and points to her car on the street out front and clicks the remote, so I can slide in the passenger side. It's a subcompact I squeeze my tall frame in. I don't mind. At this point, this little automobile is like a chariot to heaven.

We buckle up and Sharon starts the vehicle. She makes small talk including asking about the car wash and gives encouragement that I write a book based on my journal. I promise that Mrs. Schnitzer will be in my book dedication and that pleases her.

At the bus station we park, and Sharon feeds several quarters in the meter. I follow her into the same terminal from which I left when Mama kicked me out over two years ago.

The homeless man is not there that I treated so badly. Had he been, I would have stooped down and apologized for my terrible behavior and begged for his forgiveness.

After Sharon finds the ticket window, she tells the clerk she needs one ticket to Cedar's Point. She pays for the fare and then pulls another ten out of her wallet. "Here, Tony," she says. "This'll get you home…a little extra, too, in case you run into any problems."

The tears stream down my cheeks. She hugs me and says to stay strong. I thank her and promise I'll mail a copy of my book when it's published. It's the least I can do for her overwhelming kindness.

As Sharon walks away, I can't help but think about the wonderful legacy that Mrs. Schnitzer has left behind. A daughter who carries on the tradition of her mother's love and compassion and the many students—like me— who Mrs. Schnitzer influenced to be writers and who she treated with dignity despite whatever their outward appearance may be.

Every other educator at my high school wrote me off, except my English teacher.

I sit on a bench in the station and wait for the bus. Once they announce boarding, I find a window seat and fall fast asleep to a point that when I awake I'm embarrassed because I'm leaning against the older woman next to me. She didn't seem to mind.

CHAPTER FORTY-THREE

From Tony's Journal
November 13, 2015
Day 183 of Homelessness

It's Friday the 13th as I write this for those who are superstitious. Forgive the lack of a journal entry for over forty-five days. I'll explain why.

I arrived home safely and felt like I was checking into a Caribbean resort when I returned to our tent. The good mood changed, however, when I looked around and saw no cots or heater. Immediately, I wondered if James moved out although his clothes were still present.

Despite not having a cot, I collapsed on my sleeping bag and fell into a deep sleep. After a few hours, James entered the tent and gently nudged me awake. While it was a happy reunion, he had news to share. Of course, I had to tell him about the trip up north.

The inability to write was due to extra days at the car wash to generate more cash to replenish our tent furnishings and to care for James, who was struck with pneumonia. Here's all that happened.

Chapter Forty-Four

When I open my eyes, James breaks out into a big toothy grin. I smile, too. We'd missed one another. Each worrying about the other during my absence for the trip to Hell and back.

"Lots to tell ya about, James," I say.

"Yeah, me too, Tony. First, need to light my pipe." He sits down on an upright large log stump that was not in the tent before I left. Without his cot to rest on, he's obviously improvising. He lights his corn cob and I pull a cigarette out of the pack. After a few minutes of smoking, we share our tales.

"What happened to our stuff?"

"Went to the convenience store one morning, Tony. When I returned, someone had ransacked the tent. Took our cots and the little heater. Everything was overturned. I guess for kicks, they slashed a few holes in the roof, too."

I look up and see fresh patches James had made to keep out the rain. "Did the best I could to clean things up, bud."

"What 'bout my money, James? Did they get it?"

With a wink, he says, "Nah. Kept that in my shoe. A trick learned from a friend."

At least we had my savings although I knew this wouldn't be enough to replace the bunks and heater and propane canisters. *One step forward, two steps back,* I say to myself.

While the tent remained intact, we would have to re-furnish it. Another of my fears realized: that some asshole would pilfer the campsite. Before James, I traveled with my things just for this reason.

After a quick mental calculation of how much cots and a heater will cost, I know my savings won't cover what's needed, requiring as much extra time at the car wash as the owner would permit.

James waits patiently for me to recount the details of the trip.

"Where do I begin?" I say.

"How's Cassie?" he asks to prompt things along.

I shake my head. "Didn't make it. I got to see her before the priest did the last rites."

"I'm so sorry, Tony. I kept praying for you and your family."

"I know ya did. Thank you. The time up there went from bad to worse. Mama turned her back on me…literally. Mrs. Ortenzio, her nasty friend, told me to beat it in Italian."

James nods in understanding since he's been through this type of conflict himself.

"Got drunk, too. Kinda lost it." My head's down as I

say this. Waiting for a tongue-lashing although I shouldn't have been, James just isn't wired that way anymore.

In a low voice, he says, "What went down?"

"Everything just fell around me. Outta control emotions…needed an escape. Found my old man's bar and spent my whole wad on whisky and beer."

"How'd that feel?" James says, comprehending the temporary euphoria an addict receives and then tremendous guilt inevitably sets in.

"Damn good in the first few hours. Not so good when everything sank in 'bout Cassie, Mama, and losing sobriety. More than anything, I didn't wanna disappoint you." I fiddle with my cigarette lighter while I say this, not wanting to look at the only person in my life who lovingly tries to hold me accountable.

"Disappoint me, Tony? Yourself, that's who ya let down." To take the sting away, he adds, "Nobody's perfect. Been sober now a long time. I'd be lyin' if I didn't admit there were times I couldn't take life any longer, drank, and had to start over. It happens.

"You begin again and build time. Day by day, my friend. Sorry I wasn't with you."

"That would've helped at Sal's Bar, but I couldn't put you through the homeless shelter I stayed at a few nights."

"Yeah, not good places, right?"

"I don't even wanna describe the shithole it was. Well, ya know."

James grimaces at the memory of his experiences at these big city "shelters."

"Caught a cold, too. I'll try not to pass it on, buddy," I say, wiping my nose with my sleeve as I say this.

"The important thing is your home. Remember to ask God for forgiveness for gettin' drunk. He knows we're weak. The Lord understands as long as you confess it to Him."

"I did. My bunkmate up there was a veteran. Shell of a man. No life in his eyes. His situation caused me to realize mine isn't nearly as bad as his."

"Rest up, Tony. We'll talk more." I blow my nose and decide that I've got to get decongestant before the cold gets worse.

CHAPTER FORTY-FIVE

Seven days pass and I cram in as much time at the car wash as the owner allows. When I have enough saved, I ask James if he wants to walk to Walmart to purchase the cots and heater.

"Not feeling so well, Tony. If you can manage without me, I'd rather rest."

He hadn't joined me on the convenience store trip either and I noticed he was laying down more than usual during the last few days. Kneeling by him, I place my hand against his forehead. "You're burning up, James. When did this fever start?" I say.

With his eyes closed, he says, "Last night. Took a few aspirin and thought that'd help."

"We gotta get you to the hospital, bud. You don't look so good." I quickly forget about the Walmart trip. James is the priority now.

"Can you make it to the convenience store if I carry you on my back? We can't have the emergency people here since we're trespassing."

He nods weakly. I grab for a water bottle and tell him to drink up. He's looks dehydrated, too.

After we clear the tent and pipe, I kneel on the ground and guide him onto my back. James is surprisingly light.

"Alright, buddy. I'll get you to the store and we'll call 911. Get you patched up and back to normal real soon." I purposely sound upbeat although I'm worried as hell about him.

"Thank you, Tony."

It's the least I can do for my friend and tentmate. I feel guilty, too, because he caught my cold which became a more serious infection. I suspect pneumonia, or the flu has struck.

Since neither of us makes it a priority to see a doctor on a regular basis, preventive things like flu shots and routine bloodwork are not part of our regime. When you're fighting for basic survival, everything is done in crisis mode. The homeless deal with what is in front of us. Period.

The walk takes a little longer with the extra weight of James on my back. I think about the sight we must be to those we pass by. A young, tall, Italian-looking guy carrying an older, short, African American man.

Homelessness has taught me so much about human nature. The good and bad in people as they react to the poor. And more than anything the need for those on the streets to take care of each other.

At the convenience store, I put James down by the side of the building and pull my cell phone out and dial 911. I explain the situation to the dispatcher and they promise to send an ambulance.

"Wait here, James. I'll get you some Gatorade to hydrate more. Are you hungry?"

He shakes his head. "Not at all."

As I exit the shop, the ambulance and a police cruiser pull up.

The responders approach James, who is now laying on the sidewalk next to the building.

"Are ya drunk, old man?" the cop asks.

I quickly walk over and intervene. "No sir, he's sick. Flu or pneumonia. Most likely."

"Who are you?" the officer says as he gives me a quick up and down.

"His friend and roommate," I say.

"Do you have some ID?" I pull out of my wallet the card with my old address.

The cop asks if the identification is current.

"No sir, we're homeless. Steve Jones can vouch for me, if needed." I figure mentioning Dawn's boyfriend's name can't hurt. You know, cop to cop always seems to work.

"Yeah, I know him. Good man." He nods to signal we've passed safely through a potential landmine field. I'm thankful the man in blue doesn't ask for more information. I'm sure he knows there are homeless living in the woods. It's an open secret in Cedar's Point.

The ambulance crew goes to work. After taking James's vital signs and hooking him up to an IV, the crew moves the stretcher to the back of the ambulance. I ask if I can ride along with them. They don't object.

I sit at the foot of James to stay out of the way as they work on my friend. The siren blares. Off we go to Cedar's Point Memorial.

CHAPTER FORTY-SIX

From Tony's Journal
November 26, 2015
Day 196 of Homelessness

The hospital took great care of James after a few days of lots of fluids and antibiotics. While I stayed with him as much as possible, I had to look after the tent and put in a car wash day, too. Getting him back to the tent required a cab ride to the convenience store and then I carried him the rest of the way.

Before he came home, I also made the Walmart trip to purchase new bunks, a heater and propane, and I splurged on a down blanket for James, knowing the evenings would be chillier. My funds were just about depleted from these purchases.

The rest of the fall season was rather uneventful. Other than Dawn and Steve convinced Betty and Joe of Betty's Diner to take me back on a part-time, probationary basis. So, I guess that's big news. I think it impressed the owners that a law enforcement officer vouched for me.

I was honest with Dawn and Steve when Dawn called

to check on me that I'd gotten drunk during my trip up north. I assured her, however, that I had done no drugs. I won't go there. I can't go there. God help me stay sober is part of my new prayer at night besides lifting James and me out of homelessness.

Betty's Diner doesn't give me a lot of hours each week since I'm a standby busboy, but it helps along with the car wash to generate extra cash. If a full-time vacancy occurs on staff, I'm hopeful the owners will consider me.

It's Thanksgiving Day. Dawn and Steve had to travel to see his family in New York City, otherwise they would have hosted us at their table. They have become a wonderful support and it's not weird at all between Dawn and me. I'm happy for her and I think she sees a new maturity and wisdom in Tony Jankowski because of my struggles.

A church we have not been to before is hosting a free meal for the homeless in honor of Thanksgiving. We've decided to try them out. Not affiliated with any denomination, James explains they're not Catholic, Methodist, Baptist, or Lutheran, other than they recognize that Jesus is the Son of God who died for our sins.

CHAPTER FORTY-SEVEN

James and I walk to this church, close to downtown Cedar's Point. Much like my favorite Methodist Church, it's small and simple in design. Covered with darkened cedar shingles, the church reminds me of pictures of what churches look like in northern parts like Massachusetts or Maine.

Probably because of the various Maple shade trees surrounding the church that during growing season do not allow much light to shine down on the building, there's green moss all over the cedar. In late November, there are few leaves remaining on these large trees.

As we enter the sanctuary, a volunteer smiles and directs us to the social hall. Once we find that room, filled with about seven rectangular tables that have white tablecloths and place settings for eight on each, another volunteer directs us to join a table with two open seats. We recognize a few of the other diners, fellow travelers on the road that is homelessness at the Jersey Shore.

An older gentleman in a coat and tie rises at the front of the room. Gaunt, tall, and slightly hunched over, he reminds me of a picture of Ichabod Crane that Mrs. Schnitzer had hanging in her classroom—she loved Washington Irving. He proclaims himself the minister of this church.

Before we eat, he had his volunteers hand out palm cards that warned of fire, brimstone, and eternal damnation coming to those not saved. With a depiction of the flames of Hell and Satan pointing up at me, I lose my appetite and want to crawl under the table and hide.

In the minister's blessing, he prays for our repentance. This very direct approach is in great contrast to anything I'd experienced with Mrs. Seidel and in my conversations with James. This guy literally scared the hell out of me.

Dinner was served with all the Thanksgiving trimmings: Turkey, stuffing, sweet potatoes, green beans and hot rolls. For dessert, the church treated us to pumpkin and apple pie. The meal was better than anything I'd had at Maria Jankowski's Thanksgiving table. So hungry, I forget about the gruesome palm card.

As we leave the social hall, the pastor stops us. We thank him for the hospitality. He looks me right in the eyes and says, "Have you been saved?"

Startled, I mutter something about being Catholic because I don't know what else to say. As a youngster in spiritual training, I'd understood forgiveness and had renewed this prayer and been moving closer to Him in my faith journey.

The guy caught me flat-footed with his candor and the intense way he stared into my eyes when he questioned me. It was almost as if he could see into my very being. And didn't like what he saw. If only he could have seen me back in my thug days!

James then steps forward to intervene. He has no problem standing toe-to-toe with this minister and says, "My young friend knows the Lord. Thanks for feeding us, Pastor."

Pastor "Ichabod" doesn't relent and says, "We're not just feeding you, we care about nourishing your soul."

Irritated, James wants to say more but replies instead, "God bless you, sir." With his arm around my shoulder, my good friend guides me out the door.

Once we're out on the front sidewalk, I turn to James and say, "That was some scary shit, man. How do they expect to save anyone with that stuff?"

"Some believers, Tony, think it works. Unfortunately, the pastor's approach probably turned off many tonight. Let's go home."

CHAPTER FORTY-EIGHT

From Tony's Journal
December 26, 2015
Day 226 of Homelessness

James and I are sitting in the downtown library, trying to escape the "polar vortex" that has hit the region. Day one of this cold snap and we're not looking forward to hunkering down tonight in the tent with expected temperatures to be in the single digits.

No matter how much we wrap ourselves in layers, even with the little heater going, there's just no way for us to keep warm.

The library is a place to thaw and be able to use the computers and restrooms available. Some of my journal is now saved on a flash drive for when that time comes to type up my manuscript.

James is reading the Bible and the newspaper. Several other homeless men are sitting with us and at other tables also using the computers and reading. One older gentleman I recognize from the food pantry has his head down and he's sound asleep. The extreme cold accelerates fatigue.

After covering the morning shift at Betty's, I met James at the library. The car wash work has virtually ground to a halt with the frigid weather. Once a snowstorm comes along that job will pick back up with folks wanting to get the road salt removed from their vehicles.

The holiday season was quite festive in Cedar's Point. With a vibrant shopping district, people hustled about making their Christmas purchases while stopping for up-scale luncheons at several restaurants that cater to the upper income population of the area. Each of the street lights was decorated and Salvation Army volunteers collected for those less fortunate.

James and I plopped down a dollar a piece in the first bucket we passed. Lord knows we've benefitted from the generosity of not only the Salvation Army but the area's churches. James used this as an opportunity to tell me the story of the "widow's mite," and the lesson the Lord draws from her offering.

Jesus observed the rich giving their donations at the Temple. But was much more touched when a widow dropped in two coins—the entirety of her wealth. The story once again illustrates for me how much Jesus cares about the poor.

While not as destitute as the "widow" in the scriptures, we both hope our contribution pleases God.

We thoroughly enjoyed Christmas Eve with Dawn and Steve. With a nice home in Cedar's Point, Steve invited us for dinner and a candlelight service at the church they attend. Before supper, he said we could use his shower if we wanted to. Steve understands how difficult it is to remain clean for people who live on the streets.

In the best clothes we had for this gathering, what a luxury it was to have a hot shower and to then dine at a table with a fine tablecloth, cloth napkins, and a large bouquet of Christmas-themed flowers.

As we savored the ham and lasagna Dawn prepared, I watched this couple as they held hands and enjoyed each other's company. While happy for them, it was a vivid reminder of how bad I'd screwed up in the past. And a motivator for how much I want to get my life squared away so I can have my own place and a girlfriend who cares for me. And I for her.

One librarian is approaching us along with the security guard who's usually posted in the lobby. Neither of them is smiling and I've got a bad feeling about what's coming. To give them my full attention, I stop typing.

CHAPTER FORTY-NINE

"Gentlemen, you have to leave now," says the mousy librarian, empowered by the rent-a-cop at her side. Short and thin with glasses much too large for her tiny face—unlike several of the librarians who I've asked for help in using the computers or finding books—I've given "Miss Smith" a wide berth till now. Don't ask me why—other than she gives off bad karma.

One of the other guys at our table answers for the group. "Why? What have we done wrong?"

"New library policy," she says, "you're being disruptive to the other customers." I look around and see no one paying any attention to us. Scanning the big room further no customers appear to be fazed by our presence. People are browsing books and periodicals and working on computers. Just like we were.

"Disruptive? Look around, lady, we're using the computers or reading, other than my friend who's catching some sleep," our spokesman continues.

"There've been complaints about noise. I'm only doing

my job. Please pack up and the guard will escort all of you to the door."

My head wants to explode like a volcano from this bullshit. James grabs my arm to signal this is not a battle I should take up.

The brave leader of our rag-tag group can't be the only one to speak out, however. My sense of honor won't allow that. This is total nonsense and she and the wannabe cop know it.

I say, "I'm sorry but you're targeting us 'cause we're homeless. Let's call this for what it is. Do you have any idea how cold it is out there? Try to survive without heat, Miss Smith. Wouldn't last an hour out there." I slam my fist down on the desk to emphasize how unfair this is.

The guard moves menacingly towards me and says, "Come with me now or I call the police and they'll deal with you." With a prison record and only getting on my feet with the job at Betty's, I realize James is right. I can't fight this fight.

We all pack up our shit and head out the door to the lobby. I turn to James before we exit to the outside, "Now what? We can't make it at the tent. None of the churches are open today for pantries or soup kitchens. Not gonna make it out there, James."

"How much cash do ya got, Tony? Let's take a cab to the convenience store and walk back to the campsite. We'll layer up, use the heater wisely, and hunker down till this weather passes." This isn't James's first rodeo, having survived many winters as a chronically homeless man.

"Enough for a ride. That's not the point. It's just fucked up we can't hang out here and stay warm."

Normally, James would arch an eyebrow or clear his throat when I use the "F-bomb." Not now, however. I'm expressing what we both are thinking—only he's much politer, much more refined than I am.

"Agreed. But not worth the threat of the police comin'. We've both seen this kind of discriminatory crap. We keep our heads up and move on."

In a corner of the lobby so no one can see where I hold my money, from my left shoe, I pull out ten bucks and make the call for the cab. As we wait inside the atrium, the guard comes over.

"Outside, guys. Not in here." He gestures to the sidewalk out front of the library.

This time James reacts. "Young man, this isn't the end of this. There are advocates for the homeless, including the churches—and they're gonna hear about this. C'mon, Tony." In over three months of friendship, I'd never heard James raise his voice or say a cross word until now.

As soon as we open the door, a blast of Arctic air greets us. I pull my collar up around my neck and take out my wool hat from my coat pocket and put in on over my thick hair, pulling it down as far as it will go. With vinyl-lined gloves over my hands and several layers on underneath, including long johns, I'm dressed as warmly as I can.

I turn my attention to James to make sure he's bundled up. Again, I'm struck by how much older he looks than forty-nine. If he had not been homeless these many years, James could be a handsome, sturdy man. Instead of the shriveled up human being he is as he limps along and carries his magnifying glass to read anything of importance.

The cab arrives and takes us the several miles to the convenience store on Wake Street. The walk through the woods is brutal as the wind whips through the pine trees without mercy. Our eyes sting and neither of us can feel our face when we finally arrive to the culvert. I tell James to wait inside it while I start the tent heater.

Again, I ask myself—probably for the dozenth time since becoming homeless: *How can a great nation allow people to live like this? Further, how can a public facility boot out men who have nowhere else to go? Especially older, frailer men like James.*

Chapter Fifty

From Tony's Journal
December 28, 2015
Day 228 of Homelessness

The Methodist Church and several others in the area opened their doors during the day to the homeless after learning what the library had done. Mrs. Seidel texted, inviting James and me to come over the morning after the library booted us. Thank God I had given her my number.

The network of churches and homeless advocates are rising to our defense as James believed they would. Outrage is almost universal from compassionate politicians, the news media, and several outspoken humanitarians about the new library policy that denies the homeless a safe place to warm up during these polar vortex events.

After burning the tent heater for about six hours straight, we ran out of propane just before bedtime that first night of this brutal weather. The library is to blame.

We used precious fuel during the day to try to stay warm that could have been preserved for the evening—after the library had closed.

Wrapped in multiple layers of long johns and sweats and then balled up in blankets and our sleeping bags, we couldn't shake the cold. James finally suggested that we had to sleep together to allow our body heat to work off each other.

There we were bundled up and hugging one another. Not creepy or sexual or anything. Just two guys trying to survive. Despite what Mother Nature threw our way.

James even laughed at my lame joke—told at the expense of an alcoholic and addict, namely us—when I said, "Wish we had a fifth of brandy right now."

The worst part was having to go back out to the woods to piss. As a younger man, I have a much stronger bladder than James does. He goes a lot more. Still, I couldn't let him go out alone for fear he'd trip and then freeze to death.

It got to a point we stopped leaving the tent and went in an empty bottle because the effects of the wind became too much to endure. The nights are always tough but this one was the worst of my life.

Time stood still as our teeth chattered, our bodies shivered, and we got precious little sleep.

At least the canvas buffeted us from the wind. There were times, however, when I thought the tent itself might blow away and us with it.

When I got the text from Mrs. Seidel, inviting us to come over to warm up and eat, it was like a message from God. Bundled back up in street clothes, we made the walk over to the convenience store, planning on spending the little money I had left for a cab again.

To our surprise, a van was shuttling the homeless from there and several other locations to the churches that had opened their doors. In less than a day, this network of angels had organized to save those of us from almost certain hospitalization or death.

The driver had the heat blasting and thermoses of hot coffee and mugs to dispense along with donuts and fresh fruit. As James reminded me once again, "God is good."

CHAPTER FIFTY-ONE

Before we head off for the evening back to the tent, the church provides dinner. They and the homeless advocates have pooled their resources to purchase extra tanks of propane for the tent heaters so crucial to not freezing to death.

James and I settle in for the meal. Hot spaghetti and meatballs, salad, and warm biscuits. A man in his fifties sits down and introduces himself as "Jack Curran."

Tall with dark hair and a slight paunch around his mid-section, in some ways, he reminds me of a younger Tony Jankowski—only with brown eyes instead of blue. His are lined, however, with Crow's feet and streaks of gray are sprouting in his curly black hair.

Jack works hard to put us at ease, knowing there're folks we encounter that think they're better than us. After shaking hands, he says, "My wife, Carolyn, and I attend services here. Mrs. Seidel filled me in on your circumstances. I'm so sorry about how much you've struggled."

"It's not so bad after we teamed up," I say. "Without the churches open, I'm not sure we'd make it, though."

"I'm retired from a life in politics and business and we volunteer as much as we can with the pantry and other programs like this one. I'd much rather be around folks like you," he says with a chuckle, "than with the political types. Much more real I've found."

Said with no condensation, James and I sense his sincerity. I pepper him about the condition of homelessness and how a wealthy area can allow it.

Jack shrugs. "Guys, I don't have all the answers. Comin' from a city, I witnessed it. Carolyn and I took in a young man to help him get on his feet. Down at the shore, who knew there'd be homeless? Until we heard about folks like you living in tents in the woods. It sucks and shouldn't be. Since I'm not in the political arena any longer, I focus on helping as many people as I can…as one person.

"Tell me what you guys do and what you hope to become once you escape homelessness?" I like the way Jack asserts that living on the streets is only a temporary condition.

James defers to me. "I want to write more than anything. I work part-time at Betty's Diner and at the car wash over on Route 15. Not enough to sustain me, yet. James here should be on disability. Doesn't see that well and has a bad limp."

Jack's eyes sparkle at the mention of my desire to be a writer. "Me, too," he says.

"I've got some of my stuff here. Wanna take a look?"

Other than James, I've never shared my journal, a compilation of my innermost thoughts. I feel such a strong connection to Jack, however, that I slide my book across the table when he nods in the affirmative that he wants to read my stuff.

CHAPTER FIFTY-TWO

We finish dinner and Jack reads my journal as I get the three of us coffee.

I'm on edge as he turns each of the first ten pages. The hardest thing about becoming a writer is having the confidence to put yourself out there for others to critique. Only Mrs. Schnitzer and James have judged my writing ability.

After about fifteen minutes, he says, "It's raw but damn good. I wish I could write with this kind of passion and clarity. When you've got a finished manuscript, I'd be glad to be one of your readers before you publish."

"That means so much, Jack. Whatcha writing about?" I say.

"A young man's journey in politics. Only fiction... unlike yours." Jack doesn't offer to share his writing. From this brief encounter, I can tell he's a private person. A loner with a great weariness around his eyes. Almost as if he can't escape the tiredness built up over a lifetime in public service.

I want to comfort him. He has everything. A good

wife from what he says, a beach home, early retirement. *But with all this—why is he so sad?* I ask myself.

The church indicates they have to close and the homeless and volunteers pitch in to take out the trash and clean up. Mrs. Seidel and Pastor Lisa come over and hug James and me. We thank them for providing temporary shelter.

As we're packing to leave, Jack comes over. I saw him watching us intently as we moved about and then he made a phone call. There's an intensity in his eyes I hadn't seen while we talked over dinner.

"Where are you two gonna sleep tonight?" he says.

"Our tent. The church gave us more propane and we'll do the best we can," James says.

Jack shakes his head. "You're comin' home with me. I called my wife. We have a tiny guest room for our boys when they visit. They live in Pennsylvania. It's only got bunk beds. I can't let you guys go back out in this weather."

Astonished this virtual stranger would open his house to us, I guess I shouldn't have been surprised, however, since he shared he and Carolyn had brought in a young man, Gabriel, whose mother abandoned him in high school.

"That's so kind of you," James says, "but we can't impose."

"Nonsense. After this damn vortex breaks, we'll figure out next steps."

"None of our stuff is here," I say. "Everything's back in the tent."

"I'll drive you over there and you can pick up what you need," Jack says.

Mrs. Seidel is smiling as we follow Jack out to his car. He obviously confided in her about his plan. Jack unlocks a gray Chevy sedan that serves as his transportation. Simple. It's clean with no frills unlike many of the vehicles I've detailed at the car wash. Another sign this guy is a relatively common man.

Yet I can't help but think there are complications underneath that sad exterior that not too many people have been able or allowed to understand. Polite and pleasant, Jack Curran is an enigma.

He starts the car and waits until the engine has warmed up to blast the heat. "Okay, guys, where to?"

Usually we wouldn't take a stranger to our tent, but James and I exchange a glance that this can be the exception. We trust this guy and walking from the convenience store back to the campsite and back again in this weather just isn't possible because of the frigid temperatures.

"Follow Route 15 and make a left onto Wake Street and then take a right to the road that runs under the parkway. Park off the side street and our camp isn't too far from that," I say.

Jack parks the car and we walk through the woods. The temperature is dropping rapidly, and the short trek is difficult, let alone if we had made the trip from the convenience store—a much longer walk.

Jack is tall like me and he stoops down as we walk through the pipe into the tent. I'm glad we keep the place clean as he surveys the scene. "I'm sorry, guys. This isn't right in America," he says as he shakes his head with sadness.

We pack clothes and toiletries. Jack carries James's knapsack. Even though Jack is older than James, like me, he knows my friend is in bad shape for his age.

Chapter Fifty-Three

From Tony's Journal
January 1, 2016
Day 1 of Permanent Shelter

Happy New Year! Jack took us back to his house, a simple wood bungalow by the bay, only a few miles from Cedar's Point. Carolyn, Jack's wife, welcomed us at the door into their cozy home. Decorated in antiques and nautical items, it's unpretentious, reflecting its owners' personalities.

Carolyn has beautiful auburn hair and the largest blue eyes I've ever seen. Much like Mrs. Seidel, hers convey kindness, compassion, and a purity and innocence. She put us at ease even though we were strangers. After a quick tour of the cottage, we sat down in the enclosed back porch which has a view of the bay and a rooftop deck over it.

Our hosts served hot chocolate and donuts and impressed upon us two requirements: no smoking since Jack has asthma and we must keep our room clean and pitch in around the house. With a roof over our heads and gracious hosts, we immediately agreed to these commonsense rules.

After small talk and learning more about us—Jack had

Dave Transue

obviously given Carolyn a lot of background when he called her—she showed us to our room, inhabited by their rescue pit bull, JET. Neither James nor I have been around dogs before so we're a little freaked out about a pit bull. Jack assured us that JET is friendly and lovable.

The bedroom is indeed small as Jack had described it. With a bunk bed set and four-drawer dresser, a tiny closet holds linens, towels, and sheets. Carolyn had put fresh bedding on the beds and Jack suggested we stow our things under the bed since floor space is at a premium.

The bathroom is down the hall between our room and their master bedroom. Small, too, but larger than the guest room, this couple is making a go of "tiny living."

Fresh thick towels were in the bathroom for us to shower and get ready for bed. After cleaning up and changing into cleaner clothes—Carolyn had taken our dirty clothes to launder—James closed the bedroom door and suggested we pray.

We kneeled on the dark pine plank floor, which is cold since the house is apparently not well insulated. Jack had explained the cottage was originally a summer home only.

James prayed for both of us. "Lord, thank you for the generosity of Jack and Carolyn. Thank you for providing warmth, shelter, and food. God, you always take care of us and we're grateful for your faithfulness. Amen."

James cannot climb to the top bunk, so I shimmied up into it. We killed the lights and said goodnight to one another. Too wired to sleep, I stared up into the wood grooved ceiling. A street light cast enough glow I can make out the

154

age cracks. I thought about this journey of homelessness and focused on the good people that have helped James and me.

For the first time in a long, long time, I felt safe and then fell into a deep slumber. So deep I dreamed my bunk had crashed down and killed James. I awoke screaming and in a soothing voice my friend assured me he was okay.

Chapter Fifty-Four

Between that first night and the New Year, we settled into a routine, doing our best to stay out of Jack and Carolyn's way. Other than joining them for meals, we remained in the bedroom—reading, writing, and playing board games that their sons had left under the bunk beds.

I had never played Monopoly before, so James shows me the ropes. I end up beating him after he hits Park Place and the red hotel that finally bankrupts him.

Jack asks to talk with us after a huge New Year's breakfast of eggs, pancakes, sausage, and biscuits. So full, I resist the urge to go back to sleep. With the car wash shut down over the holidays and Betty's not providing any shift work, I've enjoyed a few days of rest. Both of us have cut back on our smoking, too, since it's cold out.

Over hot coffee, Jack begins. "We want you guys to stay here until we can get you on your feet. Besides the rules we discussed before, if you can help with some grocery expenses, that'd be fine. But only if you're able. The money isn't the point. We feel you guys ought to have a little stake in the household. That's all."

Stunned at this invitation to stay, James nods yes and gets misty-eyed, knowing he won't have to brave the weather in the woods any longer. He has food stamp funds to utilize.

I'm eyeing Jack with suspicion. This sounds too good to be true.

"Don't get me wrong, Jack, we're grateful. But why help us? I don't get it."

James looks over at me like I have three heads.

Jack smiles. As a former politician I guess he's seen suspicion before. "Because we've been blessed and we're in a position to help. You guys don't deserve this condition and you're doing your best to leave it.

"Look at you, Tony, you're working two jobs and you're still homeless. The boys won't be down until the summer, so the little room is open till then. I don't think it'll be that long, however, before you get settled," Jack says.

I blink away a tear at this generosity. "What can we say other than thank you? I can help with groceries, too. Least we can do. And I've got any snow shoveling covered, so you won't have to worry about that, Jack." While he's a strong guy in his fifties, I'm becoming protective of him like I did with James. Losing Papa while I was so young apparently never left my subconscious.

"Carolyn and I have a friend who is a terrific advocate for the homeless. She's had tremendous success with housing placement and will put James in touch with people who will help with a new disability application."

James cries as if a huge weight has been lifted from

his hunched over shoulders. I reach over and put my arm around him.

"We'll get in touch with your friend right away," I say.

"Already done," Jack says. "Her name is Eileen, and she's comin' over this week to begin the process. You'll like her. She takes no prisoners in how she blows through the bureaucracy but cares passionately about helping people get off the streets.

"Eileen also has lots of contacts to put people into rehab, but you guys say you're clean. I see no evidence to doubt that." Jack obviously has volunteered enough around the homeless to watch and observe for signs of addiction.

"James has been sober for years now. I had a relapse with alcohol when my sister died back in September, but I've been clean from drugs since I went through rehab in prison."

Comfortable enough to mention prison again, during dinner at the church and the follow up conversation the first night we spent with them, I made sure I owned up to my record with both Jack and Carolyn. Neither of them seemed to be threatened by it, understanding I was a first-time offender, imprisoned for metal theft and drug possession.

JET has been watching James and jumps up to lick him in the face. An amazing dog, he senses how emotional my friend is. James pats JET on the head and laughs. This is the first time I've seen my buddy truly smile. A smile of joy and relief.

Chapter Fifty-Five

From Tony's Journal
June 14, 2016
Day 166 of Permanent Shelter

This journal ends at the location where it began: one year after I started chronicling this journey. At the pier in the Cedar's Point harbor, I'm leaning against a piling. Only this time I'm not alone.

Nestled against me is my girlfriend, Krissy. That's right, you read it correctly. I…have…a…girlfriend! I want to shout it from the rooftops. I want to take out a blazing headline in the Cedar's Point Tribune. I want to rent one of those planes to pull a banner at the Jersey Shore to let the world know I'm in love.

Krissy is the best thing to happen in lots of good things to happen out of the depths of despair that is homelessness.

Small and petite, Krissy has strawberry blond hair, usually pulled back in a ponytail, except for bangs that run evenly across a freckled forehead. Although I've never met a farmer's daughter, she reminds me of what one looks like. Wholesome, but fun.

We met at Betty's Diner when I was busing tables. Krissy had just finished a piece of peach pie with whipped cream on top. A blob was stuck on the tip of her pert little nose. I couldn't help myself but laugh. Krissy joined in, breaking into an infectious smile that envelops her whole being.

Against the backdrop of a perfect summer day with a blue sky and white clouds, I introduce Krissy to my seagull friends as they dip and soar. "Those are Frankie, Jane, Virgil, and Carol," I say as I point to them.

She laughs at my imagination and I recreate for her the scene one year ago, including the sailboat with the beautiful women who beckoned me to join them.

With a punch to my arm, she says, "I hope you didn't jump on board."

As serious as I can muster at a moment like this, I deadpan, "Nope, I was saving myself for just you." Krissy laughs again. And then we kiss, tenderly, passionately, as if there's no one else in this harbor. Or on the planet. Time stands still, and I am content and grateful.

I treat her like a queen and I am proud to be her knight in shining armor. To feel a warm, loving body snuggled against me while I sleep is the definition of perfection.

Only a year apart in age, Krissy is studying graphic arts at the community college. An artist, too, she's painted a watercolor of me I cherish, capturing the happiness I have found at this stage—after twenty-four years of what has been a difficult life. Until this year when James and I found shelter, and I met my girlfriend.

Krissy is a practicing Catholic. When I can attend Mass with her I do so, rediscovering my faith in Catholicism. The rituals and liturgy I learned as a boy now bring comfort and order. I'm mature enough now to understand the Church has been a consistency throughout these many centuries and one I can lean on, along with my Savior.

With a gentle breeze blowing off the ocean and no humidity, it's a perfect day. The salt air is a natural perfume. Unlike in the past, I am clean, and my clothes are clean, and I don't have to be ashamed or worry about being chased away as a "societal misfit."

This peaceful setting is a good spot to reflect on these past few months when everything crystalized. With no boats moving about while Krissy and I look out at the harbor, the water sparkles like thousands of diamonds dance on its surface. I lose myself in thought looking at this delightful image.

True to his word, Jack introduced us to Eileen. Tall and strong in appearance with a pretty face and shoulder-length black hair, her personality matches her personal strength. Eileen indeed takes no prisoners when it comes to helping the homeless.

Her eyes have such an intensity, I've said more than once to Jack and James, I'm glad she's on our side.

Bureaucrats know not to throw up needless obstacles in front of her. Eileen goes around or barrels over them in a focused quest to end homelessness in Cedar's Point.

After about three months of living with Jack and Carolyn, Eileen found us subsidized housing—a rooming house near downtown with two open rooms and placed us there.

With her assistance, the government approved James's disability application, and he receives a monthly stipend that allows him to pay his reduced rent. Along with food stamps and the pantries, he can survive without having to live in a tent.

Betty's hired me full-time after I proved myself while on probation. Sundays are reserved for worship at the Methodist Church since I've got a loyalty to them from the food pantry they run that helped save me during my darkest days.

And in a somewhat ironic twist, I help at the pantry as Mrs. Seidel's runner, grabbing items from the shelves for each order she fills. I see the destitute folks we're serving and my heart breaks for them.

I see no conflict with my going to Mass, too, since I don't take communion with the Methodists. Something Pastor Lisa says she understands.

I detail cars after church. Between these two jobs, I'm able to afford the subsidized rent and have saved over four hundred dollars so far. My goal is to buy a used auto once I've saved enough.

Although I work seven days a week—other than time off for church service, Mass, and the food pantry—I don't mind. I am gaining self-sufficiency and have a new self-esteem, thanks to the many people who helped rescue me.

The rooming house where we live is clean. On each floor is a shared bathroom and kitchen. James is on a different *floor but that's okay. He's safe and we take the bus over to worship together, joining Mrs. Seidel and Jack and Carolyn in their pew.*

Although small, my room feels like I'm living in a penthouse in Manhattan. I love the coziness. It's become the place where I'm comfortable and motivated to finish this book.

Let me introduce you to my little slice of heaven. Heated with a painted radiator and cooled in the summer with a small window unit, there's a twin bed along with a red maple dresser and white desk and chair.

I've splurged and purchased navy blue curtains with anchors to frame the one window which looks out onto an alley. For me, the view couldn't be better. It's all mine. Instead of an alley filled with trash cans and parked cars, I see mountains, rainbows, and the horizon stretching out over the Atlantic Ocean.

I can't be around the sea enough. And hope this summer to take a day here or there for my girl and me to hang by the sea. With my hair much longer now, I'm sporting a man bun and my physique has filled out with a healthier and steadier diet than during those days when I ate lots of carbs and starch.

I hope to show off what a handsome couple we truly are as we walk along the beach. At this point in my life, after the humiliation I suffered as a former homeless man, I hope you can indulge this touch of ego.

My new prayer each night, as I rest my head in safety and warmth is: "Dear God, thank you I'm no longer homeless. I pray for all those on the streets. For their physical, mental, and emotional needs. I pray for their wellbeing. Help them escape...as you helped me. Amen." And then I render the sign of the cross.

While my journey was difficult, I'm one of the blessed ones. Many homeless people struggle with addiction and repeated times in and out of rehab. Many have untreated mental illness. Many can't shake the despair and hopelessness that comes from this condition of drifting with no home to call your own.

I dedicate this to Mrs. Schnitzer and her daughter, Mrs. Seidel, James, Dawn and Steve, Jack and Carolyn, Eileen, Krissy, and, most of all—to the Lord, who saved me from sin and from the perils of the streets.